"Aaaaah!"
A scream ca...
from somewhere ouside.

"What was that? That's not in the plan!" Wishbone said.

Another yell came from deep in the night's darkness.

"Joe!" Cassy said. "What was that?"

Joe gulped. "I don't know," he said. "It sounded like a scream."

"I know that! But where do you think it came from? And who was it? And why?" Cassy asked. "I sure wish Officer Krulla hadn't left."

"Just when I was getting cozy," Wishbone said, "Oh, well. This is what I was trained to do. Let's go Joe."

Joe dropped the book he was holding and stood up. "I'm going outside to investigate," he said.

Books in the
WISHBONE™ Mysteries series:

Books in the **WISHBONE**
SUPER Mysteries series:

*coming soon

PHANTOM OF THE VIDEO STORE

by Leticia Gantt

WISHBONE™ created by Rick Duffield

Big Red Chair Books™ *A Division of **Lyrick Publishing**™*

This book is a work of fiction. The characters, incidents, and dialogues are products of the author's imagination and are not to be construed as real. Any resemblance to actual events or persons, living or dead, is entirely coincidental.

 Big Red Chair Books™, *A Division of* **Lyrick Publishing™**
300 E. Bethany Drive, Allen, Texas 75002

©1999 Big Feats Entertainment, L.P.

Edited by Kevin Ryan

Copy edited by Jonathon Brodman

Continuity editing by Grace Gantt

Cover concept and design by Lyle Miller

Interior illustrations by Al Fiorentino

Wishbone photograph by Carol Kaelson

Library of Congress Catalog Card Number: 99-64027

ISBN: 1-57064-587-6

First printing: December 1999

10 9 8 7 6 5 4 3 2 1

Printed in the United States of America

To Mom

FROM THE BIG RED CHAIR . . .

Oh . . . hi! Wishbone here. You caught me right in the middle of some of my favorite things—books. Let me welcome you to the WISHBONE Mysteries. In each story, I help my human friends solve a puzzling mystery. In *PHANTOM OF THE VIDEO STORE*, my best pal, Joe, and I work at a video-rental store during winter break. Business goes on as usual until a vandal tampers with some of the videotapes. Joe and I must discover who the culprit is before the store loses money and customers, and is forced to close.

The story takes place in the winter, during the same time period as the events that you'll see in the second season of my WISHBONE television show. In this story, Joe is fifteen, and he and his friends are in the ninth grade. Like me, they are always ready for adventure . . . and a good mystery.

You're in for a real treat, so pull up a chair, grab a snack, and sink your teeth into *PHANTOM OF THE VIDEO STORE!*

Chapter One

Wishbone walked back and forth in front of The Movie Shoppe, Oakdale's video store. It was a beautiful, crisp Friday afternoon in December, perfect weather for a game of fetch.

But Wishbone wasn't in the mood. The white-with-black-and-brown-spots Jack Russell terrier was a little worried about his best friend, Joe Talbot. Joe was inside renting a movie to get his mind off the fact that he didn't have a part-time job during his unexpected break.

Usually, Joe would spend most of his free time after school hours practicing and playing basketball for Wilson High School. But several days before at practice, while he was taking a charge, he fell backward. He tried to catch his balance but ended up with a sprained right wrist. The injury was going to bench him for a few weeks. He had to wear a bandage around his wrist, too. So the team coach released Joe from practice until his injured wrist could have enough time to heal.

Although Joe was disappointed not to be able to practice, he decided to make the most of his time off. With the holidays coming up, he had wanted to earn extra money to buy presents. Joe had talked to his mom the night before about getting a job.

Joe doesn't need to buy me anything, Wishbone thought. *A scratch—or two—behind the ears will do.* But the dog knew that Joe had more expensive gifts in mind for the others on his list.

That day, right after school, Joe and Wishbone had gone to Rosie's Rendezvous Books & Gifts. Joe had worked there the last summer. Wishbone and a talkative parrot named Mr. Faulkner had been the official mascots of the used-book store.

Joe assumed the owner, Mr. Gurney, would hire him on the spot. Instead, Mr. Gurney told him he hadn't expected Joe to work during the holidays. He knew Joe played basketball and assumed he would be practicing. Mr. Gurney had already hired all the extra help he would need for the season.

Mental note, Wishbone thought. *Don't count your chickens until they're hatched . . . or your pizzas until they're delivered!*

The dog caught the smell of pepperoni drifting on the chilly wind. It came, he suspected, from Pepper Pete's Pizza Parlor, just down the street. And it smelled as though a pizza was headed right his way.

That's the answer—Joe can work at Pepper Pete's. And I'll get all the side benefits—a doggie bag every night!

The terrier sat down outside the video store and imagined the possibilities. Pepperoni and mushroom. Pepperoni and green pepper. Pepperoni and extra cheese . . . At that moment, someone walking toward him from the distance caught his eye. It was unusual that a person could tear Wishbone away from his pizza dreams. But this wasn't just anybody.

She walked with determination toward the video store, carrying an armful of books. The terrier knew almost everyone in town, but he didn't recognize her. Taking a big sniff of the cool air, he hoped his excellent sense of smell would give him an I.D. He caught the aroma of cookies—the scent was full of possibilities.

Wishbone greeted the stranger immediately as she got close to him. "Welcome to Oakdale! I'm Wishbone. But before I tell you any more about me, let's discuss cookies. You like 'em? You make 'em? You have 'em?"

She bent down and patted him on the head. The scent of the cookies came so close to Wishbone that he could almost taste them. He could barely stay still. "Hey, little guy! I think I know why you're so happy. Bet you'd like one of these, wouldn't you?" She pulled out a bag of cookies from her backpack and opened it. Much to the terrier's delight, she broke off a large piece of one for him. "My mom made these for me this morning," she said.

In between chews, Wishbone said, "You wouldn't happen to have another piece you could spare, would you?" But the girl had already gotten up to go into the video store.

"Joe! Joe!" The dog raised himself up and put his paws

on the front door. He tried to get his best friend's attention. "Forget the video—ask her for a cookie! They're delicious!"

Joe had been standing near the store's entrance. He was looking at some of the newer videos for rent. He turned around when he heard the entrance door open. When he had gone inside a few minutes before, the store seemed to be empty. The only sound he heard was a police chase. It came from a movie playing on individual TVs throughout the store.

The place had changed a lot from the last time he'd been there. High shelves were still everywhere, fully stocked with videos. But now, big cardboard cutouts of movie characters and posters of alien-fighting heroes decorated the store. The store had looked pretty dull before. The place now also smelled of fresh paint and new carpet. It was lit up so brightly that he had to squint as he ran his eyes along the shelves. A video caught his eye and he took it off a shelf.

He looked toward the door as it closed. He saw a girl approaching him. He immediately forgot all about movies. Joe smiled at her, curious. He had never seen her before.

"Hi!" she said. "How are you?" She stopped in front of him after setting her books down on the checkout counter.

Joe was surprised that a girl he didn't know would just strike up a conversation with him. But her friendliness came as a pleasant surprise. She seemed to be a few years older than he was, maybe nineteen. Her curly, shoulder-length brown hair framed her green eyes. She was almost as tall as Joe.

He ran his hand through his straight brown hair, pushing it away from his face. He didn't answer her question, so she took a look at the video he was holding.

"That's a great movie. I just saw it the other day—for the fourth time. I laughed so hard my stomach hurt," she said. "Or maybe it was from all that popcorn I ate. Anyway, it's a great film. You'll love it. Not that I know you well enough to predict your taste— Well, I don't know you at all, but I can just tell you'd love it." She smiled. Then, when Joe still didn't say anything, the girl bit her lip. "By the way, my name's Cassy. So, what do you think?"

Joe wasn't quite sure what the question was. Before he could even try to give any answer, the entrance door opened again. Both he and the girl turned toward it.

Joe watched as the girl's friendly expression changed.

A tall, lanky blond boy about nineteen years old walked in with a pizza box. He was singing along to the music coming from his headphone set. Joe had seen the boy working at the video store before.

"Oh, yeah!" the boy sang out, unaware that he now had an audience.

"Ed!" Cassy said loudly. After that remark didn't catch his attention, she yelled. "Ed!"

The boy looked surprised and removed his headphones. "Whoa! Cassy! You're back!"

"I got back this morning. Where have you just been?" she said angrily.

That's why she was talking to me, Joe thought. *She must work here.* He sensed that there was some tension between the other two people. He pretended to be interested again in the videos that were on the shelves. Looking at the shelf in front of him, he couldn't help but overhear the conversation.

"You went out to get a pizza? I left you in charge while I was in California seeing my mom, and this is how you've been handling your responsibilities?" She shook her head in disbelief.

"The pizza place is just down the street. I was super-hungry, and I couldn't wait for it to be delivered." Ed set the pizza box down on the counter. He pushed it toward Cassy. "I got extra anchovies. Take a slice if you want one."

Cassy didn't.

"I'll share," he added, looking from Cassy to Joe. "Come on, have a piece."

Joe shook his head no. He couldn't believe that Ed was behaving so irresponsibly.

"Would you stop talking about the *pizza!* How about the store? I come back to find this kid all alone in here," Cassy said angrily.

Joe wasn't happy to hear her refer to him as a "kid."

"Hey, calm down. What was I supposed to do? I was starving. It's not like I wasn't coming back," Ed said.

"We've been through this before. If you have to work alone during lunch or dinner, either bring your food and eat it here, or order something and have it delivered. At the very least, you should have locked the doors when you left," Cassy said.

"This is Oakdale, Cassy, not some big, crime-ridden city! Besides, when Stan and Margie owned the place, the rules weren't so strict. Ever since your mom and you took over, it hasn't been as much fun to work here." Ed hopped up on top of the counter and stuffed some pizza in his mouth.

Joe remembered that Stan and Margie Miller used to own the store. Now the store's new look made sense to him. Cassy and her mom must have remodeled the place after they bought it.

"I can't believe you're talking to me like this," Cassy said. She closed the pizza box and handed it to Ed. "Now, please leave. You're fired."

Ed jumped down from the counter. "Relax! I just went to get a pizza."

"Watch yourself, Ed," she said. "You've pushed me too far. If this had been the first time something like this happened, I might think about letting this incident go. But this is your last mistake—here, at least. Now, take your food and yourself out of here before I say something I may regret later," she told him.

Ed finally realized Cassy was being serious. "Chill out. This place isn't so great, anyway. Besides, I've got better things going for myself," Ed said. Joe admired Cassy's ability to control herself. At that point, he was struggling not to say something to Ed himself. Ed picked up the pizza box and headed for the door. Then he turned around suddenly and faced Joe. "Watch out for her, pal. She's tough," he said sarcastically. "Really brutal." He put his headphones back on and left the store.

Joe and Cassy watched in silence as Ed walked off and then disappeared out of sight. Then the girl turned to Joe,

her face red. "I'm so sorry you had to be part of this. If I seem too upset, it's because I'm really tired. I just got off a plane. Then this whole incident with Ed didn't help, either. But I promise there's not nearly that much drama going on here," she said with a sigh.

"He was out of line," Joe replied. He caught a glimpse of Wishbone standing outside the window, barking in Ed's direction. He wondered if it was the pizza or just Ed's attitude that had caught Wishbone's attention.

"Yes, he was. You know, the previous owners, Stan and Margie, described him as an ideal employee," she said. "But they were so wrong. Ed worked here when he was a student at Wilson. Now he is a film student at Oakdale College. This was a perfect job for him. Too bad he messed up." She looked around the store. "Unfortunately, that leaves my mom and me with exactly one employee—me. We've been open only one week. With only two employees, we've cut back the hours until we can find more help. But with just one person working, we may as well shut the doors."

Joe thought about asking to take over Ed's job. His luck, which had started out badly that day, now seemed to be taking a turn for the better. Working at a video store would be a dream job. He could learn a lot about movies. Practically the whole town, including all his friends, stopped by the store. He'd be able to recommend videos to the customers. And Cassy seemed pretty cool, too.

"You know, if you need extra help around here for the next couple of weeks, I could come in after school, on weekends—" Joe began. He stopped talking when he realized how nervous he sounded.

"Really? You need a job? That would be great," Cassy said, looking excited.

"Yes. And don't worry. I'm nothing like Ed," he replied. "I mean, not that Ed's a bad guy, but, well—"

"You don't have to explain anything to me. I know exactly what you're trying to say." From her expression, Joe knew she did. "But having you work here—that would be great." She paused. "I'll have to get a reference, though," she said, as she took off her jacket and walked behind the counter. "Where's the last place you worked?"

Joe had been a camp counselor, but he had done that as a volunteer. Joe had had only one job for which he had earned a salary. "Last summer," he said, "I worked at Rosie's Rendezvous Books and Gifts."

"With Mr. Gurney? What a coincidence. I was just there," Cassy said. She pointed to the stack of books she'd set down. "It's such a great store. I stop by there all the time. Do you like to read? Well, you probably do, since you worked there and all. . . ." She paused and frowned, wrinkling her forehead. "Wait, why aren't you working there if you need a job?"

Joe explained how he hadn't planned to work over winter break until he hurt himself. Then it was too late.

Cassy looked sympathetically at his wrapped-up wrist. "Ouch! I'll bet that's pretty painful. First you can't play basketball, and then you can't find a part-time job. But that may be solved with one quick phone call," she said. She thought for a moment. "I guess you can handle videos and work the computer with one hand. I certainly don't want you to hurt your wrist any further. Excuse me for a minute."

She reached for the telephone on the counter and dialed Mr. Gurney's number from memory. While she spoke with him, Joe looked around the store, amazed at his stroke of good luck. He couldn't believe how well his situation was turning out.

Cassy hung up and laughed. "Mr. Gurney gave you nothing but the very best reviews. And these I trust, one hundred percent. With all that praise, I'm surprised he

15

didn't try to hire you again," she said. "But there's no way I'll give you up. Mr. Gurney said that your working conditions involved a package deal—something about 'Wishbone'?"

Joe smiled and pointed outside. "Wishbone—he's my dog. If you don't mind having him along, of course. He actually helped out at the bookstore."

"Mr. Gurney mentioned that, too. Now I understand why Mr. Gurney was laughing when he spoke of a package deal." Cassy turned to look at the dog. He was eagerly pressing his nose against the window. "Of course he's welcome here. This store could use a canine touch. And he loves my mom's oatmeal-raisin cookies. She's in California. She baked me a batch right before I caught my flight to Oakdale. I gave him a piece of one before I came in," she said.

"Then you've already won him over," Joe said.

"Great! You'll start tomorrow, Saturday. We open at eleven o'clock sharp. The store hours are Monday through Friday, eleven to six, and Saturday and Sunday, eleven to seven. We'll discuss your hours later. And just wear jeans and a T-shirt. We dress very casually here. I'll have to get you one of our store's logo shirts. Now, how about that movie you were looking at earlier? Do you still want to rent it?"

Joe certainly didn't need the film to cheer him up anymore. But he thought that his mom might enjoy watching it. Besides, renting the film would give him the chance to get a better feel for his new job.

Chapter Two

"The home stretch!" Wishbone said as he raced alongside Joe to the Talbot house. Now that Joe had found a part-time job, the dog could relax and enjoy the rest of his Friday evening.

"And it's come down to the wire! Wishbone's in the lead, with Joe close on his tail, and the winner is—" The dog raced up the driveway and slid to a halt. "—Wishbone! By a nose!"

Joe stopped his bike beside Wishbone and laughed at the panting but happy dog.

"Don't take it so hard," the terrier told Joe. "You put up a good race. But two wheels versus four paws—well, you can do the math."

Wishbone turned to look at the house of his neighbor, Wanda Gilmore.

"Good! I'm glad you guys saw that," he said. The pink flamingoes and the toucan on the mailbox that decorated her yard stood at full attention. "I run a pretty impressive race, huh, guys?"

Wanda, who was busy on a ladder hanging up her holiday lights, saw the pair arrive. "Hello! How did everything go at the bookstore?" she called out to them.

Joe told her that Mr. Gurney didn't need any holiday help.

"And?" Wishbone prompted his pal. "Isn't there a little more to the story?" He barked and wagged his tail. "If only they'd listen to me! I always tell the good stuff first."

Wanda climbed down from the ladder and walked toward Joe. "What?" she asked. "He doesn't need any help?" she said, a deep frown on her face.

Her look of dismay changed as Joe told her excitedly about the job he had been offered.

"I *love* movies!" Wanda nodded with such enthusiasm that Joe and Wishbone couldn't help but nod along. "It feels wonderful to be curled up on the couch, with a bowl of popcorn, and a whole other world just a Play button away."

"I hear you, Wanda. And that's got me thinking, guys," Wishbone said. "I'd say somebody needs to capture *my* life on film. It's really quite interesting, you know. Documentary-style would work best. Of course, we'd need an action-cam, because you'd be amazed at what my days are like. I'm thinking a trilogy—a three-part series."

While Wishbone was busy imagining what actor would play him, Wanda came over to the Talbots' yard. She had begun to walk with Joe toward the house. "Guys . . . guys?" Wishbone said, running toward them.

He caught up with the other two on the front porch. The terrier walked through the doorway of the two-story wood-frame house.

"One day, this place will be famous," the dog continued. He headed toward the couch in the study, where Wanda and Joe had removed their jackets and sat down. The dog sniff-searched for his squeaky toy. "This spot, for instance, will be remembered as the place where Wishbone stashed his treasures," he said. He got between Joe and Wanda and pulled the squeaky toy out from between the couch cush-

ions. Then he turned to his favorite area in the house, maybe even in the world—his big red chair. He set his toy on the chair. "This will certainly be bronzed," he said, as he leaped up and sat down.

At that moment, Joe's mother walked into the study.

"Ah, hello, Ellen!" Wishbone greeted her. He got off his chair and sat in front of Joe. "Wait till you hear about our day. *And* we brought you a movie—to celebrate our good fortune."

Ellen Talbot was an attractive woman in her thirties. Like her son, she had dark brown hair and was tall and slender. She sat down on the arm of the couch, next to Wanda, and asked Joe, "So how did everything go at the bookstore?"

As usual, Wishbone spoke up before anyone else. "Not too great, but thanks for asking. We do, however, have an exciting prospect in the movie business," he said. As usual, no one listened to the dog.

Joe quickly explained all about the bookstore and his new job. Ellen seemed quite surprised by the turn of events. "Don't Stan and Margie Miller own the video store anymore?" she asked.

Wanda answered. "They *used* to own it, but they recently sold it. I've tried to get in touch with the new owner, to welcome him or her to Oakdale, but I haven't been able to yet. Her name is right on the very tip of my tongue. . . . What is it, Joe?"

"Actually, I'm not sure," Joe said, fidgeting in his seat and looking at his hands. "I didn't get to speak to Cassy for very long. Her mom, the owner, is still in California. I don't know when she'll be back," he admitted.

"It makes me a little uneasy that we know so little about the two, and that you've never met your employer," Ellen said. "I'd like to stop by tomorrow and meet Cassy, but I'm working all day at the library."

"Oh, trust me, Ellen, Cassy's great," Wishbone said. "And I can promise you that her mom is an exceptional person. I've seen proof, even eaten it—delicious, mouthwatering, raisin-enhanced proof."

Joe told his mother that she had no reason to worry about Cassy. Although he had spent only about fifteen minutes with Cassy, she seemed very nice. But Ellen still looked concerned.

"Don't think about it another second," Wanda said, as she patted Ellen's knee. "I'll stop by tomorrow on my way home from *The Chronicle* and introduce myself to Cassy. I need to know her—we're practically business-district neighbors!"

Joe tried without success to convince Wanda that she didn't have to go out of her way.

Wanda acted as the eyes and ears of Oakdale. She owned *The Oakdale Chronicle*, the town newspaper. She was also involved in many local organizations, from the Arbor Society to the Oakdale Historical Society.

"Some things in Oakdale remain a mystery even to you, Wanda," Wishbone said. "Things in your own yard, in fact. Second hydrangea to the left of the porch? I buried a sock underneath it just last week."

Ellen invited Wanda to stay for dinner and watch the movie he had rented. She accepted.

After eating and watching the film, Wishbone relaxed in the living room with his three friends. "Dinner was great, guys," he commented. "But the movie was missing something. The director failed to show us the all-important canine point of view."

His opinion, however, belonged only to him. Ellen and Wanda loved the film. Joe laughed throughout the movie, so he obviously enjoyed it. When the movie was over, though, Wishbone noticed Joe looked a little upset. The terrier knew it wasn't from the pizza they had for dinner, or the film, however.

"A little nervous about the new job?" Wishbone asked. He could usually guess what was bothering his best friend. He put his paw on Joe's leg. "How about a snack? That always makes me feel better."

Suddenly, Joe said he was going upstairs to bed.

Wishbone followed his buddy up to their room. "What? Turn in so early? This isn't quite the superstar lifestyle I dreamed of," Wishbone said. "But I've had my bit of cookie and pizza, so I really shouldn't complain."

Joe wasn't thrilled that his neighbor was going to stop by the video store to check on him. He was fifteen years old, in high school, and could make some decisions on his own.

He didn't want his mom and his neighbor friend to worry, though. If it would make them feel better, he wouldn't complain.

He went into his room and shut the door after Wishbone had followed him in. After grabbing a small ball off the floor, Joe tossed it at the hoop that hung on the back of his door. And, as usual, he made the basket. He found it comforting to do something so familiar. Tomorrow, at the video store, he would be doing exactly the opposite—entering entirely new territory.

Wishbone nuzzled against Joe's leg.

"You'll help me tomorrow, won't you, boy?" Joe asked, as he patted his dog on the head. "We already know how Cassy feels about you."

Joe got ready to go to sleep and then climbed into bed. But when he tried to fall asleep, he couldn't. He kept going over the events of the day in his mind. He wondered if he seemed too young to Cassy to work there. Of course, she had hired him. Joe hoped Cassy truly felt he could handle the job.

Joe debated the issue for about five minutes. Wishbone, meanwhile, lay snoring peacefully at his feet. Finally, Joe turned on a light and got out of bed. He rummaged through his closet, deciding what to wear the next day. Fortunately, his favorite blue shirt was clean. He would wear that shirt until Cassy gave him a store shirt.

Suddenly, he felt Wishbone nudge his leg. All Joe's movements had awakened the dog. The terrier stared at his friend with a puzzled, sleepy-eyed expression.

"I know, boy," Joe said, as he walked over to his bed and turned off the light. "It's time for me to go to sleep."

He lay down, and Wishbone returned to the end of the bed and yawned. Looking at the clock, which glowed a bright red 11:30, Joe realized how late it was. Luckily, he found Wishbone's yawning contagious and was soon fast asleep.

Chapter Three

"I never thought I'd say this, Ellen," Wishbone said, as he headed toward the front door Saturday morning. "But I think we're skipping breakfast. Joe got up really late and spent a little too much time getting ready for work."

Wishbone and Joe were almost out the door when Ellen handed Joe a brown-paper bag, his jacket, and his backpack.

"It's chilly outside. And the bag has two blueberry muffins," she explained. "For the road." She looked at Joe's wrist. "Are you sure that you can handle the bike all right with your sprained wrist?"

"I'll be fine, Mom," Joe said, as he slipped the bag in his backpack.

"How about a few more, Ellen?" Wishbone asked. "It's a mighty long road this morning."

But Wishbone didn't fool her. The Movie Shoppe was not very far away.

Joe rolled his bike out of the garage. He hopped on it and headed to work. The ride to the video store—Joe on his ten-speed, Wishbone trotting beside him—was a fast one. "Wow! Could we slow it down?" the dog asked, as he panted beside Joe. "I haven't had my muffin yet."

By the time they reached the video store, even Joe was out of breath.

They arrived fifteen minutes early, just as Stan and Margie Miller were walking out of the shop. "Good morning!" Wishbone said. But the couple didn't return the greeting. In fact, they were both frowning. *They must not have eaten breakfast yet, either,* he thought.

Joe tried to open the door, but it was locked. He saw Cassy inside and knocked to get her attention. She waved and came to let him and Wishbone in. Then she locked the door behind them again.

"Good morning!" she said. "I'm glad you're here early. We've got lots of work to do."

Wishbone immediately began to sniff around the store. He considered it his first duty of the day to track down more oatmeal-raisin cookies.

"I just got here a few minutes ago myself," Cassy said. "Stan and Margie, however, were waiting outside for me. Ed spoke to them last night and they wanted to convince me to re-hire Ed."

"Yikes!" Wishbone said. Cassy's comment distracted him. He temporarily forgot about the cookies that he'd just uncovered.

Cassy noticed the dog's rummaging. "You already found them in my backpack, did you?" she said playfully.

"Forget the cookies—at least for now. What about Ed? You didn't listen to Margie and Stan, did you?" the dog asked.

Cassy looked at Joe, expecting a smile.

But Joe frowned. "So they came here to talk to you about Ed?" he asked.

"Oh, no way would I re-hire him." She had guessed what he was going to ask next. "In fact, I was a little upset they had interfered. They gave me and my mom some important advice about running the store when we first bought it. But what they've done now is definitely out of bounds," she said.

"Whew!" Wishbone said with a sigh. "Now, about these cookies . . ." He rummaged some more.

Cassy smiled. She bent down and pulled out a bag of cookies from the backpack that was sitting on the floor. She opened it, then handed a cookie to the dog.

"Put your backpack behind the counter, Joe," she said. "I'll show you around the store. Oh, and here is your store shirt. There is a restroom in the back where you can change."

Joe thanked her.

"I'll join you shortly, after I enjoy my cookie-and-muffin breakfast combo," Wishbone said. He had found the muffins in Joe's backpack. "No better way to start the day."

Cassy and Joe began at the front of the store. There were two counters—a long one and a short one—with a computer sitting at the end of each. All the work on computers was done there. Cassy booted up the two computers. She explained that customers checking out videos would stop at either counter to pay and then walk between the two counters to the exit door. A third computer, and VCR and TV monitor, sat in a far back corner at the long counter. Joe had no idea what they were for.

"As you can see," Cassy told Joe, "the Movie Shoppe has two doors—an entrance and an exit on either side of the long counter. That's to make sure no one can walk out with a video until they check it out at the counter. Hidden sensors are located by the exit door. They will set off an alarm if anyone tries to sneak a tape out," Cassy explained.

"Impressive design," Wishbone commented. "But where's your doggie door?"

Beyond the front counter, the rest of the store was full

of shelf after shelf of videotapes. The movies were divided into sections by category: Kids, Action/Adventure, Mystery, Drama, Comedy, Science Fiction, Horror, Documentary, Musical, Foreign, and History. Along the walls were the new, most popular movies.

Wishbone searched all over for the Animal Action/ Adventure movies. "Cassy, you can't tell me this category doesn't exist! All the great directors have tackled this theme," he said. "I promise that I'm going to protest against this oversight!"

"Now," Cassy said, "we're going into 'the back.'"

"Oooh! I hope 'the back' includes a 'snack room,'" Wishbone said eagerly.

Cassy, Joe, and Wishbone walked along some rows of shelves. Then Cassy opened a door in the left rear corner of the store. There was another room, about half the size of the one out front. This one was undecorated and had no carpet. Large metal filing cabinets lined the walls, and there was also a row of file cabinets in the middle of the room. Cassy led her new employees inside.

"This room is for storage. In the far left corner," Cassy said, pointing to a door at the back of the room, "is the restroom. At the far right corner is the office. You can place your backpack in the office. That's where we keep all the money. We keep a lot on hand to make sure we always have change for the registers. There's a phone in there, too, if you need to make a personal call. I like to keep the phone up front free for business calls. Once we open the store for daily business, we lock the door to this storage room. I'll show you where an extra set of keys is kept up front."

Cassy walked with Joe to one of the filing cabinets and opened the top drawer. Empty, flattened video boxes were stuffed inside it.

"We take new tapes out of their original packing. Then

we put them into plastic cases that have our store logo and a unique bar code that identifies the videos. We buy lots of copies of the most popular movies. We rent them as many times as we can. Then we pack them back into their original boxes. We then shrink-wrap the packages, sticker them with the sale price, and they're ready for the previously viewed movie bin, where you can buy them at half price."

"I never knew there was so much to running a video store," Joe said.

"Neither did I. And there is a lot more, but for now this is enough," Cassy said, laughing. "My mom and I have never done this kind of thing before, either. Stan and Margie showed us how to do just about everything."

Cassy and Joe hadn't noticed, but Wishbone was several file cabinets away from them. He was staring at the open bottom drawer of a filing cabinet.

"Are my eyes playing tricks on me?" Wishbone said in a dreamy voice. "Could this possibly be real?"

Cassy and Joe turned their attention to the dog—and to the boxes of candy he was drooling over.

"These are snacks that we'll be selling at the counters up front," Cassy explained. "I take credit for this idea—sugar is my biggest vice."

"This was your idea?" Wishbone said. "Cassy, you're a genius. *Please* let me work on this project. I'll take full responsibility for the candy inventory. I'll put my acting career on hold."

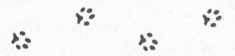

"Great idea," said Joe. "How'd you ever come up with it?"

What a goofy question! he thought. *Cool, Joe, real cool.*

"Thanks, Joe," Cassy answered. "I noticed that some other video stores sold candy, so it's not really my own idea. Maybe we can put the candy display together today," she said. "Now let's get to work. Why don't you take your backpack to the office and change your shirt before we open?"

Five minutes later Joe returned. Cassy flipped on a switch. This switch, located by the front counters, controlled a master VCR that played the movie that was being shown throughout the store. The TV screens that were all over the store awoke with a buzz. "We try to open at the same time each day—eleven A.M.," she said. "All my college classes are early in the morning, so I can usually get here by then. Until my mom returns, our working hours will have to be flexible, depending on when each of us is available. It's just you and me, you know."

"I'll be here as much as I can," Joe said quickly. "After Tuesday, I'll be off for the next two weeks for winter break, so then I can work all day. Once school starts up again and my wrist heals, I won't be able to work."

"Two weeks will really help. I'll be able to find someone else by then. And I'll be glad to have you around," Cassy said. "Now, for the most enjoyable duty of the day— choosing what film we'll play on the monitors. It has to be G or PG, though. You and I may be old enough for R-rated films, but not all our customers are."

She thinks we're about the same age! Joe thought. *Should I tell her?* He knew he had to. He cleared his throat and said, "Actually, Cassy, I'm just fifteen," he said.

"No way! You look so much older!" she replied.

He blushed. "Nope, I'm just fifteen."

"Well, then, no R-rated movies for you, either," she teased. She selected a movie and inserted the tape into the master VCR.

Cassy headed over to the short counter to a cabinet that was connected to the night drop-off slot. The drop-off slot was located outside the store. She slid open the cabinet door. About thirty tapes poured out.

"Welcome to Video Store One-oh-One," she announced. "First we check in all the movies that customers returned while we were closed. There is another drop-off slot located on the side of the counter by the entrance door."

Cassy sat down on the floor and picked up one of the videos.

"Open up the plastic case. Then make sure the movie title we've put in the case matches the name of the movie on the video label inside." She pointed to a printed label inside a plastic sheet on the case. "And check to make sure the tape is rewound. After you've checked them all, take them over to this computer," Cassy said. She walked across to the long counter to a computer in the far corner. Next to the computer was a VCR and monitor. "Then zap the bar code into the system using this handy zapper." She picked up a handheld scanner. She scanned in a tape, and the machine beeped. "That lets the computer know the tape has been turned in. And that's it! The video is ready to go back on the shelf for its next rental."

"What if the tape isn't rewound, or if the label doesn't match the name on the box?" Joe asked.

"If the tape isn't rewound, rewind it on this VCR." She pointed to the VCR and monitor sitting next to the computer on the counter. "But your second question's a challenge. If it's one of our movies, the customer probably just rented more than one and mixed up the boxes. So just check all the boxes and switch them. But if the tape's not one of ours, it might be one of the customer's own videotapes. Sometimes people accidentally return those to us. Or it could be a tape from a different video store. You may need to call the customer to come pick up the tape and return the correct one. All customer phone numbers are in our computer database."

"Seems pretty simple," Joe said.

"Glad you think so," Cassy said. She walked to the front doors and unlocked them. "We're officially open for business now. While you're handling the returns, I'll go get the money to open the registers," Cassy said. "Holler if you have any problems!"

Joe went after the pile of tapes on the floor with enthusiasm. His first job was to check them in. To carry them to the computer, he stacked a big bunch on his uninjured arm. Holding them against his body, he stood up slowly to keep his balance. But as he headed to the computer, which was near the entrance door, a loud alarm went off.

Startled, Joe dropped a few tapes. When he tried to pick up those, he dropped the rest of them. The sound of the hard plastic boxes hitting the floor made almost as much noise as the alarm. Cases opened up, and tapes fell everywhere.

"Oh, no," Joe said, as he dropped to his knees. He hoped Cassy hadn't heard all the commotion. Working as fast as he could, he began to put the tapes back in their cases. Wishbone came over. With his muzzle, he pushed the tapes toward Joe.

Cassy returned to the front counter. "Well, what I just heard wasn't quite a 'holler,' but somehow I knew—" She noticed the pile of tapes and Joe's worried expression and stopped teasing him. "Don't worry about it. Dropping a big stack of tapes was my initiation into the video-store world, too. And I should have told you," she said. "You don't actually have to walk through the sensor system to set off the alarm. Sometimes if you just get too close it'll go off."

Cassy looked down at all the tapes Joe had dropped. "And maybe try carrying fewer tapes at once next time,

31

especially with your wrist injury. Ironically, thirteen is the magic number—the most I can carry at one time. It's tempting to try for those few extra tapes. But one mishap a day will convince you otherwise."

No more mistakes today, all right? Joe said to himself. With the videotapes stacked up neatly, Joe picked up exactly thirteen and carried them to the counter. Wishbone scooted the remaining ones over with his muzzle.

Cassy smiled. "Joe, I knew Wishbone would be a great asset to the atmosphere here. As to whether your dog could physically help out, well, I had my doubts. But now I know better."

Joe smiled and patted his dog's head. "He's always surprising me, too."

As Cassy began to head toward the back room, Wanda Gilmore walked in.

"Hi, Miss Gilmore," Joe said, as he scanned in a bar code with the zapper gun. The machine went crazy and beeped wildly for about five seconds.

I couldn't possibly have dropped all of the videocassettes and also messed up the computer system in just minutes, could I? Joe thought.

"Oh, my," said Wanda, holding her hand to her mouth. "Press Escape and Shift. I think that'll solve almost any computer problem."

"No!" Cassy came running back to the counter. "That will close out the program."

Joe moved out of Cassy's way. He hoped she hadn't noticed how red his face was.

She explained as she typed on the keyboard. "When it beeps like that, it just means that the tape you scanned in is overdue," she said. "If you type in Control and Return, the account name will come up on the screen."

The name "Damont Jones" popped up in huge letters.

"Wow! It's five days late, for a total of ten dollars in late fees. This will not be a happy customer," Cassy said.

Of all people, Joe thought, *why does my first problem have to be with Damont?*

"Damont's not always in a good mood to begin with," Joe said.

"You know him?" Cassy asked. "Well, if he comes in today, let me take care of him. It's hard to charge your friends a late fee. Definitely too much for your first day. I can't have you quitting on me out of frustration."

"I wouldn't exactly call Damont a friend," Joe said. "We play on the same basketball team together."

Cassy faked a shot. "Did I mention I'd perfected the layup? I never miss," she said. "Well, actually, I'm horrible at basketball. But I can soothe the pain of a late fee any day. So if he comes in, let me know," Cassy said.

Joe smiled. Then he realized Wanda was still waiting patiently at the counter.

"Oh, Miss Gilmore, I'm really sorry for making you wait," Joe said.

Wanda immediately got down to business. "I'm Wanda Gilmore, and I'm on the Oakdale Welcoming Committee," she explained to Cassy. "We're very happy to welcome you to our town," she said. "And we'd like to take you and your mother to lunch. What day would be good for you?"

"It's nice to meet you, Miss Gilmore," Cassy said. "My name is Cassy Bennett. I'm sorry, but my mother is unavailable. Without her here, I wouldn't feel right going out to lunch. It's her store, really. Besides, I've been a student at Oakdale College for a semester now. I'm really not new in town."

Wanda wasn't content with the girl's responses. "Oh, well, when will your mother return? I hear she's in Los Angeles. And, I don't like to be rude, but I've forgotten her

33

name. Joe, his mother, and I were talking about her last night, but I couldn't quite remember her name." Wanda looked at Joe and winked.

Does Wanda have to say that we were talking about the store last night? Joe thought.

"Her name is Beth Bennett," Cassy finally said. "And I'm not sure when she'll be back, actually. She's in California, but not in Los Angeles," Cassy said, as she turned her back and rearranged some papers on the counter.

But Wanda went on in her ever-bubbly tone. "Ooh—that's it! I just couldn't remember her name last night. Neither could Joe—"

"Actually, I don't think Joe could have known what her name was," Cassy said, as she turned and looked at Joe. "I don't think I've told him that."

Joe gave Wanda his most desperate look. *Maybe now Miss Gilmore will change the subject,* he hoped.

"Where in California? You know, I went on a trip to Sacramento a few years ago and fell in love with the place," she said.

Joe shifted uncomfortably back and forth on his feet as he watched Cassy's face. She didn't look happy.

"Yes, California's a great place. Great," Cassy said flatly.

Wanda finally sensed Cassy's discomfort. She stopped asking questions. Joe sighed in relief.

"Well, let me know when your mother arrives. Now, I'd like to rent the new movie with that older film star with the gorgeous eyes. What's his name again?" she asked.

"Peter Robinson? Oh, he's so nice and funny. He's also a great cook. You're right, he has the most wonderful eyes," Cassy said, apparently forgetting the earlier uncomfortable conversation.

Wanda's mouth dropped open in surprise. "You *know* Peter Robinson?" she asked.

Cassy suddenly looked ill at ease again. "Did I say that?" she asked.

Joe and Wanda both nodded yes.

"I meant to say he *seems* like he'd be nice, and I read in a magazine that he enjoyed cooking," she added quickly. Walking over to a nearby shelf, Cassy brought back the video she knew Wanda had referred to. "Here it is," she said, smiling at Wanda. "And I'll teach Joe how to check out a movie with this transaction—if you don't mind being his first official customer, of course."

"I'll know I'm in good hands," Wanda said.

Cassy asked to see her video store card, but Wanda didn't have it with her. So Cassy told Joe to type in "get gilmore, wanda" to pull up the account. "If you didn't know her, you'd ask for an I.D.," she explained. "Sometimes people rent on accounts they aren't authorized to use—like their friend's, for example—and then rack up late fees."

Joe followed Cassy's instructions. He scanned in the bar code.

"It's all in the computer database," Cassy said. "All the info about this tape—when we got it in the store, how much it cost the store, the rental fee, who's rented it before—is stored right here."

Wanda handed Joe four dollar bills after he told her the fee. He entered the amount into the computer. The sum of seventy-five cents popped up on the screen. Next, the cash drawer beneath the counter popped open. Joe handed Wanda three quarters and thanked her for her business. "That's due Monday before closing," he said.

Cassy was impressed by what she had just seen. "Joe, you handled this transaction very well."

Joe smiled.

"He will impress you in many ways," Wanda said. "He's a smart kid."

There's that word again, Joe thought. *Kid!*

"Even as a baby, he caught on to new ideas so quickly," Wanda gushed. "You should have seen him! Oh, my, was he cute! Still is, in fact," Wanda said, as she nodded at Joe.

Joe couldn't believe his ears.

"Don't worry, Joe," she said. "First days are always a little difficult. You just hang in there." Wanda patted him reassuringly on the shoulder.

Out of the corner of his eye, Joe could see Cassy smiling. He was too embarrassed to look at her directly.

Before Cassy could stop Wanda, the woman started to leave through the exit door with her movie.

Beep! Beep! Beep! The alarm went off. Wishbone began to bark.

"One last thing to learn," Cassy told Joe. "Don't hand videos to customers right at the counter. Put outgoing movie rentals here." She pointed to a shelf right by the exit door. "That way they won't set off the sensor alarm." She waved good-bye to Wanda as she left the store.

For a few minutes, no one else entered the store.

"Appreciate the slow time when you have it. It can be crazy in here sometimes," Cassy said.

"That sounds like good advice," Joe agreed.

"Let's update the board," Cassy said. She pointed to the "Upcoming Releases" sign that hung on the wall behind the front counter. It advertised new movies that had just come in, plus those that would be released soon. "We usually update the board on Tuesdays, when the new releases come in. That's a pretty interesting day, too. People will drop by and ask for the new movies before you can even put them out on the shelves. And if there are more customers than you have videos for that one movie, watch out."

A few minutes later, Joe was alone at the counter. His two best friends, Samantha Kepler and David Barnes, came in, carrying a large pizza.

Samantha, or Sam as her friends called her, worked part-time at Pepper Pete's Pizza Parlor. She also participated in lots of activities at school—photography, drama, and the newspaper. And she was always ready for a soccer game or in-line skating.

David kicked a ball around sometimes himself. He was more likely, though, to be found behind a computer or in a laboratory. He was scientific by nature, very logical, and a good problem-solver. Although just a freshman in high school, like Joe and Sam, David sometimes worked on special projects at Oakdale College. He had brown eyes and curly, short dark brown hair, which was under a baseball cap today.

"Lunchtime!" Sam announced.

Joe smiled upon seeing his friends—and freshly baked pizza. He had called them last night to tell them about his job. But he wasn't sure how Cassy would react to his taking a lunch break so soon after he arrived to work this morning. He hesitated, then said, "Sam, David, thanks, but you didn't have to do this for me."

"We didn't," Sam said, laughing. "This is a delivery for Cassy."

"Joe, who don't you know in Oakdale?" Cassy asked. "I ordered us a pizza to celebrate your first day on the job."

Joe was shocked that Cassy had thought to do that. "Wow!" he said. He watched her as she walked across the room toward them.

"Hi, I'm Cassy," she said. "Two people to deliver pizza?"

Sam and David introduced themselves. Sam explained that her father owned the pizza parlor. David was a good friend and had come along for fun.

"Well, please join us. I think there's enough pizza to go around," Cassy said. But then she remembered the dog at her feet. "Then, again, I don't know how much Wishbone will eat. We may have to order another." Cassy smiled at Joe. "I'll go get us some soft drinks from the back," she said, as she walked away.

"Wow! Joe, what a cool boss," Sam said.

"She's great," David added.

Joe nodded his agreement.

The three friends chatted while they waited for Cassy to come back. Suddenly, Damont walked in. Joe let out a sigh, but he was a customer. "Hello, Damont."

"So, Joe, you've gone from selling books to hawking videos," Damont said. "And you've brought your little dog with you, too. Did you think you'd need help putting the tapes back on the shelves?"

Sam, David, and Joe were used to Damont's sarcasm. They knew the best way to deal with it was to ignore it.

Cassy came walking up to the front of the store. She put down the soft drinks and touched Joe's shoulder. Joe realized that she must have heard the brief exchange as she was coming from the back of the store. "How's it going?" she asked Joe, looking at him and then at Damont.

Damont's super-cool attitude occasionally failed. This time, when Cassy looked over at him and she smiled, it completely cracked.

Swallowing the gum he was chewing, he started to cough. Then his face turned red.

"Are you okay?" Cassy asked. She seemed genuinely concerned.

"Yeah, yeah," Damont said, catching his breath. "I was just telling Joe how cool it must be to work here."

"Well, thank you, Damont," she said.

"Yeah," he continued. "And maybe if you need more help, I could work here, too."

David and Sam looked at each other in alarm. But Joe stayed calm. He knew Cassy well enough to know she wouldn't do that.

"Well, Damont, thank you for the offer, but no. Joe's handling the job really well. I don't think we'll need your help. But please come by and rent movies anytime," she offered.

"Yeah, sure," Damont said. He left the store without saying another word.

Cassy punched Joe's arm teasingly. "You didn't tell me that Damont was so cool."

And on top of all this, Joe thought, as he grabbed a slice of pizza, *I'm actually getting paid, too!*

Chapter Four

The slender, gray-haired man with glasses was insistent. "No, lad! You cannot help me. I must speak to your manager immediately. And please hurry. This is not how I intend to spend my Sunday afternoon!"

Wishbone pleaded with the angry man. "Let us just *try* to help you. This is only our second day at work, and yesterday went so well. Please!"

The man looked down at the dog with disapproving eyes. "You allow canines in here?"

Wishbone used his teeth to grab a candy bar from a shelf in the front counter. Joe had helped Cassy display the candy Saturday afternoon. "What if I offer you a snack? It's on the house. Would that help smooth things over?"

Leaning across the counter, the man forced Joe to give him all his attention. "This animal has a confection in his mouth. This must violate a number of health codes, not to mention personally offending me," he said in a huff.

"I'm sorry my dog bothers you," Joe apologized.

"Come on, Joe! I was just trying to be friendly," Wishbone said. "Besides, you know the old saying: 'Never trust a person who can't be bribed with candy.'"

"Cassy should be back shortly," Joe told the man. "She's the manager."

"I'm acquainted with Miss Cassy Bennett," he replied. "But perhaps Ed is here. He has helped me in the past."

"No, sir, there's just me. And again, if I can help you with anything—" Joe began to say, trying one last time to calm the man.

"No, you cannot. I'll wait," the man said.

Joe and the unhappy customer spent a few minutes in an uncomfortable silence. The man fidgeted with his glasses and adjusted his tie and tweed coat. Wishbone, meanwhile, continued to check out the candy display. Yesterday, when Cassy and Joe had put it together, Wishbone had supervised.

"I'm thinking that maybe the chocolate-covered raisins need to be moved. They just seem wrong next to the gumdrops," Wishbone said. "Is it just me?"

No one answered. Fortunately, Cassy returned before too long. Wishbone knew she'd have an opinion.

The man turned on her the moment she walked in the entrance door. "Where is your mother? I want to see your mother," he said.

"Oh, Dr. Meacham," Cassy said, trying to balance her textbooks in her arms. "My mom is not available. But I can help you." Cassy set her books down on the counter and approached the man.

"Joe and I tried to help, Cassy," Wishbone said. "I even offered him a snack."

"I would prefer to talk to the elder Miss Bennett directly," the professor said with a sigh. "But you shall have to do. It's about this." He removed a videotape from his briefcase and handed it to Cassy.

"I rented this movie, *Fool's Gold,* yesterday," he explained. "And this morning, when I went to play it, I found that someone had tampered with it!"

41

Cassy looked at Joe, who shrugged his shoulders.

"What do you mean—" she said, slowly taking hold of the video.

"Oh, here!" Meacham interrupted her. He took the tape out of her hands. He looked around, then said, "Follow me." He led them to the VCR and monitor on the counter. He ejected the tape that was in the VCR, put his in, and pushed Play.

The movie played on the monitor for a few seconds. Then the picture disappeared and the screen went blue. After a moment, the campus of Oakdale College appeared on the screen. Then the focus zoomed in on a window at the school. Joe saw his friend David adjusting a television. He was wearing shorts, a T-shirt, and sneakers—not his usual winter work outfit.

Cassy recognized David immediately and looked at

Joe. "I wonder what this is about," she said, completely puzzled.

They soon found out. David stood up and started marching in place. Then he began to jump around and box the air. The camera zoomed in again and a close-up of David's face appeared. His face soon became drenched in sweat.

Wow! Wishbone thought. *Look at him go!*

"I think the young man is doing kick-boxing, or some similar kind of nonsense," Dr. Meacham said. "And we do *not* offer a class in kick-boxing at our college facility."

"Oh, Dr. Meacham, let me apologize for this. I don't have any idea of how those scenes got on to the movie tape," Cassy said.

"And let me emphasize again that I had no part in this tape vandalism—other than being the victim, of course," Dr. Meacham said sternly.

"I don't know how this happened. To make up for all this, I'll give you another copy," Cassy offered. "And for all your trouble, you can have a free rental the next time you visit us."

The offer seemed to be acceptable to the professor, and he began to leave the store. But once more he spoke of his disapproval about having Wishbone on the premises.

"I'll take that into consideration," Cassy promised halfheartedly.

"I certainly hope you will," he said as he turned and left through the exit door.

Wishbone walked up beside Cassy. "You were just saying that, right? I promise that in no way do I violate any health code standards. I'm very clean."

"Sorry, guys, but I had to tell him something that would satisfy him," Cassy said. "He's in charge of the film department at the college, and he rents a movie here almost every day." She started to chew on her fingernails. Then she said, "How did David get on this tape? This is so bizarre. Joe, will you scan this?" she asked, as she handed him the video-tape. "I want to know how much it's going to cost the store to replace it. We have only two copies."

Joe frowned and informed her that the tape cost one hundred dollars.

"Why couldn't this have happened to a cheaper movie?" Cassy said in frustration.

"Why is it so expensive?" Joe asked.

"Videos that companies expect to sell a lot of copies of are priced inexpensively—at fifteen or twenty dollars. They're called 'sell-throughs,'" she explained. "But less-popular movies, like this little historical drama, are more expensive. The movie companies know only a few copies will be sold. Since they plan to reproduce only a small number, their price per video is higher. If you want to buy this movie, you'll spend a hundred dollars."

Wishbone tried to make Cassy feel better. "This candy concept is going to go all the way through the roof. I predict we'll make a hundred dollars on it before you even know it. If I had any money at all, I'd start buying the snacks here immediately."

"What a way to ruin a perfectly good Sunday after-noon," she said. "How could this have happened?"

"A mystery! A case needing to be solved! Joe and I are *so* right for this job. We *do* have a little experience in the mystery-solving field," Wishbone said.

Joe decided that he would do everything he could to help find out what had happened to the video. "First, let's check and see who rented this film before Dr. Meacham did," Joe told Cassy. "It should be in the database, right?"

Cassy nodded.

Joe pulled up the information on the computer. "No one has rented it before," he said. "Two copies were shipped here last Tuesday. Dr. Meacham's the only renter so far," Joe said. "That makes him the prime suspect, right?"

"He's an unusual person. But it wouldn't make sense for him to do something like this—it would be too obvious," Cassy said. "But, for now, let's put his name on the list of suspects."

"Now let's call David and find out when this tape of him was made," Joe said. He called the Barneses' house to try to track down his friend. David's mom told Joe that David was over at Oakdale College working on a special project. She gave Joe the number where he could reach his friend.

Joe quickly called David and explained the videotape mystery to him.

David, extremely curious to know more, left the college and raced over to the store in less than ten minutes.

"That was quick!" Cassy exclaimed. "I can never make it from there to here in less than fifteen minutes."

"It must be all those workout routines you've been doing," Joe said.

David laughed. "I hear there's a must-see video starring me," he said.

Joe played the video for David to see.

After watching the tape, David explained. "That was just yesterday about three o'clock in the afternoon. I'd been sitting at a computer at the college for a few hours and was feeling a little groggy. The professor I work for suggested I get some exercise by working out to a new aerobics tape she had. I felt a little weird, doing aerobics in the office, but it really brought my energy level back up." David laughed as he moved his arms up and down above his head, as if he were doing a jumping jack.

Joe looked at his friend strangely. Wasn't David embarrassed? *I can't believe he keeps his cool around Cassy, especially after seeing himself do aerobics,* Joe thought.

"Yesterday was the first time I did this routine," David said. "Someone must have just videotaped me without my realizing it."

"Wow!" Joe said. "How could our culprit take the video after the doctor rented it, tape you, then get it back to the doctor without anyone noticing?"

"Our criminal must be very quick and sneaky. And whoever it is has access to Dr. Meacham's house, his office, or his briefcase," Cassy said.

"But someone may have seen the person videotaping David," Joe said. "David, did you notice anything unusual when you were at the college yesterday?"

"No, not at all," David said. "And it could not have been an accident. It would be too much of a coincidence if someone accidentally took the professor's tape, accidentally taped over it with me in it, and then accidentally returned the tape to the professor."

"It's awfully creepy to think that someone's been spying on you. And whoever it is is costing me and my mom lots of money," Cassy said. "I'd like to think it was an accident, too. But I agree, it's just too much of a coincidence."

Cassy's comment, and the sigh that followed it, made Joe more determined than ever to solve the case. "I think I saw a glimpse of a hand at the end of the segment with David in it," he said. "That might be the person putting the video camera's lens cap back on."

Joe quickly rewound the tape. Playing it again, this time in slow motion, he did notice a hand.

"It looks like a man's hand," David said, as he squinted at the screen.

"You're right," Joe said. "And there's a glimmer—maybe a gold ring? Does anybody else see that?"

"Maybe," Cassy said. Joe felt her shoulder touch his as she leaned in to try to look from his angle. "But it's awfully blurry."

"You know, there's a lot of high-tech video equipment in the film department at the college," David said. "Maybe if we take the tape there, someone could play with it. Then we might get a clearer picture."

"Great idea," Cassy said. "But guess whose permission we'll need to use their equipment?"

Joe frowned.

"That's right. Our good friend, Dr. Meacham," Cassy said in frustration. "Let me do the honors, please. Hopefully, he'll be at the number we have in our database."

She found the number and called. It took her a while, but she convinced the professor to see them the next day. The professor could see them only at seven-thirty in the morning. They agreed. That would give David and Joe until eight-thirty to talk to the professor. With fifteen minutes to spare, they could still get to the high school by eight-forty-five for first period. Cassy could not go because she had an early class.

Chapter Five

Monday, bright and early, Wishbone made sure his collar was on straight. *You never know when you might be discovered,* he thought. His short experience in the movie business—at least in the video-rental business—convinced him that he had the qualities to become a star. His was an untapped market—canine adventures told from a dog's point of view. And there, on the Oakdale College campus, he just might run into someone who'd recognize his great potential. The dog leash was not part of the plan, but Joe insisted.

Joe, Sam, and David walked with their hands in the pockets of their jackets, behind Wishbone. They had a different goal on campus: their appointment with Dr. Meacham. Joe had called Sam yesterday after dinner. He'd invited her to come along.

The terrier admired the red-brick buildings that surrounded him. *Possible movie idea:* Wishbone Goes to College, he thought. *This is the perfect setting for it!*

There were few people on the campus. Not many people had classes so early in the morning. And, to the dog's disappointment, none of the few people walking around seemed to be Hollywood types. The night before, Wishbone had thought of a list of items to make him appear like a star:

- *Sunglasses. Even if it's cloudy. Worn even if indoors. Gotta find some canine-sized shades.*
- *Muzzle-to-tail black clothing. I'm not wearing any kind of silly costume, though. There is a limit to what I'll do to become a star.*
- *Cellular phone. So I can order a pizza anytime, anyplace.*
- *Super-cool attitude. Say things like "Let's do lunch." A phrase I hope to hear often.*

As he looked around, the terrier's sense of disappointment grew. Two students threw a ball to each other across the mall. Another sat bundled up, reading a book.

Suddenly, Wishbone heard hurried footsteps behind him. A glimmer of hope came to him. *Maybe a talent scout is so eager to talk to me that he or she is running to catch up,* he thought. Then, sadly, the fellow just ran right past him.

Wishbone tried not to lose all hope. Many actors had worked hard for years before getting their big break. He'd been trying out only for a short time.

Okay, the next person is going to give me my lucky break, he thought with all his canine will. But a guy who looked as if he'd just rolled out of bed leisurely walked by, eating a bagel.

If he's not a Hollywood bigwig, at least he appreciates a good breakfast, the dog told himself.

By the time Wishbone and his friends reached the building where the film department was located, the terrier had pretty much given up on his great dream of being "discovered" in his hometown.

Like Lassie before me. Well, I guess I'll just have to head for Hollywood, he thought.

He'd begun to pack his bags mentally—squeaky book, a few of Ellen's homemade cookies, a pair of Joe's socks to remember him by—when it happened.

She walked by.

He saw her approaching from far away. A Hollywood type? She didn't meet any of his qualifications—she wore gray, not black. A baseball cap hid her hair. Wishbone saw no phone, and she waved to the ball players as she walked by.

Hmm . . . the dog thought. *She looks familiar. Have I seen her at Beck's Grocery, perhaps?*

As she got closer, Wishbone knew that wasn't it. When she was only a few steps away, he remembered—the video store, aisle four, shelf three, teenaged comedies. *Her name— what's her name?—she's a star! And she's about to pass right by me!*

The dog stood still and wagged his tail. He struck a pose. Then he continued walking. He was so busy looking at her that he didn't notice the broken tree branch.

Thunk! He tripped and skidded a few inches.

"Wishbone, are you okay?" Sam asked.

"Cute dog," the girl said as she came by.

Wishbone looked up at the sound of her voice. *I know that voice—it's Hilary Morgan Cooper! Star of* The Last Day of School! *And she thinks I'm cute! Wowza!*

He recovered from his fall and gazed at the girl, ready for her to announce his big break. But close up, he realized the girl just *looked* like Hilary Morgan Cooper.

Darn! he thought. *It's not her, after all.*

Joe knelt down and tied Wishbone's leash to a bike rack. They'd reached the front of the film building—

Wishbone's final stop. Joe didn't even want to consider the idea of taking him into Dr. Meacham's office.

"We're going to see the professor, so wait here, okay?" Joe said to Wishbone. "We'll be back in a few minutes."

The three kids headed into the building. They were early for their appointment with the professor. "Joe, why didn't Cassy meet us here?" Sam asked.

"She's got a test this morning," Joe said.

"And I thought that students finally got to sleep late in college," Sam said.

"She takes her classes early in the morning," Joe explained. "She goes to school here only part-time and is done before eleven o'clock. That's why she can work at the store during the day."

The three walked up the small, narrow stairs to Professor Meacham's office. Joe knocked on the door, but no one answered. He knocked again.

"Yes! I hear you! And I'll be with you in a minute," an irritated-sounding voice answered. Joe recognized the voice immediately.

The three sat on a bench beside the door. They sat quietly for a few minutes. David looked at his watch. Joe tapped his foot and Sam started humming. She stopped suddenly.

"I wanted to ask you a question last night when you called, but I forgot. What is Cassy's mom like? Do you know anything about her?" Sam asked Joe.

Joe hadn't learned too much about Cassy's mom. But he did know a little. "Miss Bennett is in California. This is the first time she's owned a video store. I'm not sure what she did before." Joe tried to think of something to add. "She makes great oatmeal-raisin cookies. At least Wishbone seems to think so."

"You don't say," a voice said from behind them. They

51

turned to see Dr. Meacham standing in his doorway. "I wasn't aware that dogs typically ate cookies."

The group stood up quickly and turned to face the professor. "Sorry, we didn't know you were waiting," Joe said.

"I wasn't. You're early, and I see you've brought another friend along. You told me a David Barnes would be present, but who is this?" The doctor looked carefully at Sam and David. "Thankfully, however, your canine companion is elsewhere."

David and Sam looked uneasily at Joe.

Maybe I should have warned them about the professor's attitude, Joe thought.

Joe introduced his friends. The professor ushered them into his office. Shelves of books lined the walls of the dusty room. The only signs of the twentieth century were the movie posters that decorated the upper parts of the walls, a phone, and a TV and VCR. A large wooden desk dominated the small room. The man sat down behind it. Sam and David sat in two old side chairs. Joe leaned against a book case at one of the walls.

"Let me begin," the professor said, "by establishing one point. I am doing this as a favor to Cassy's mother. I admire her work."

Her work? Joe was curious about the remark, but the professor didn't explain.

The professor turned to David. "I am aware of your activities on campus, which recently seem to consist of some rather frivolous goings-on," the professor said. He peered sternly at David from behind his glasses. "Although I'm permitting you to use certain facilities here on campus because of your work with one of my colleagues, in no way do I consider my allowing you in here to be an invitation to use my department's facilities or disturb my staff on a regular basis. And I'd appreciate some assurance that I'm not giving shelter to truants. Are there no classes at Wilson High School today?"

"Sir, our classes don't begin until eight forty-five," Sam explained.

Meacham tapped his fingers on his desk. "Good. You should be finished here in ample time to get to school," he said.

Joe waited a few seconds as the professor turned and looked out the window. *Maybe he's searching for the right words,* Joe thought. But soon the silence in the room grew uncomfortable.

"Sir," Joe said softly to draw his attention. He reached into his backpack, pulled out the corrupted videotape, and handed it to Dr. Meacham. "This is your tape from yesterday. I viewed it several times, and I thought I noticed someone's hand at the edge of the picture. I hoped we could make it out more clearly on your equipment."

The professor didn't respond. Instead, he buzzed someone on his speaker phone. It squeaked loudly.

Someone answered cheerfully, "Alex, here."

"Please come to my office regarding the matter we discussed earlier this morning," the professor said. He finished the call and turned to Joe. "If you'll excuse me for a moment, I have another matter to attend to," he said. He got up and, taking the video with him, walked out of the room.

"He sure is strange," David quietly said to Joe.

"A little unusual, I agree," Joe said, as he rested his arm on a bookshelf behind him. "But it's cool that he's going to help us."

Joe's weight placed too much of a strain on the shelf he was leaning on. One half of the shelf popped up, like a seesaw. Books tumbled down onto the floor.

Sam got out of her chair and quickly started picking up books. "Hurry! Let's put them back in place before the

professor returns," she said. "Or he might think we were snooping around."

The three kids picked up the books. As they were stacking them back on the shelf, Joe noticed a videotape labeled "12/18 #1."

"I wonder what this is," he said, pointing to the video-cassette. "This is the day you were taped, David."

But before they could do anything else, Dr. Meacham reappeared with a man in his twenties. Joe assumed it was Alex. His tall frame loomed over the professor's. Alex dressed casually. He wore jeans, with a wrinkled flannel shirt over a T-shirt. He seemed laid-back and relaxed in contrast to Dr. Meacham, who was strung as tight as a guitar string.

"Alex, this is Joe, Samantha, and David. Please help them for no more than twenty minutes. Then return to the project that you and I were discussing earlier. Remember, that project *must* be finished by this afternoon." The professor tapped his watch face. "That will be all," he said. He returned the tape to Joe, then dismissed the kids with a wave of his hand.

Following Alex toward a room down the hall, the three didn't say a word. Alex turned to them and laughed. He saw the looks on their faces. "Guys, guys, I'm just his teaching assistant. Relax. I'll feel awkward, otherwise. And besides, I'm looking forward to seeing this tape."

David spoke up. "It's pretty strange."

"You're the star of it, right? I hear you have a pretty dangerous roundhouse kick," Alex responded. "Why would someone tape you without your knowledge? What would they gain?"

"I thought about that last night," Joe said. "It was either a prank to embarrass David, or to get back at the store. If it was to embarrass David, they would have to know him well enough to know if something like that would bother him. If they are getting back at the store, they would have to know something about the movie-rental business. It'll cost the store one hundred dollars to replace the video."

"That seems to make sense. I understand a prank, but why would anyone want to do anything bad to the store?" Sam asked.

"I don't know," Joe said, as Alex came to a stop at the end of the hallway, then opened a door and walked inside. The kids followed.

The room felt about fifteen degrees colder than the hallway outside. Glowing computer screens provided the only light. Alex asked Joe to close the door behind them.

"A little chilly, huh?" Alex said. "The editing machines get really hot. We keep this room cooler than everywhere else to prevent them—and us—from overheating. Keep your jackets on." He motioned for the kids to pull over some chairs.

They sat in front of a desk with three monitors and a keyboard of instruments and dials. CPUs and hard drives sat in an open-faced cabinet beside them. Everything appeared very high-tech, except for the bag of chips and soft-drink cans scattered on the desk.

"Snacks, anyone?" Alex said. He held up a bag of candy.

"A little early for me," Joe said. "But, thanks, anyway."

"Well, then, go ahead and pop your tape into the third VCR over there," Alex said. "And let's see if we can figure out who our perpetrator is."

Joe put the tape in and pushed Play. Alex watched it closely.

The tape ran for about twenty-five seconds, and then suddenly Joe cried out, "There! That's it!"

Alex stopped the tape. Using one of the dials, he turned the tape back to the scene Joe had pointed out.

"Yep! That's a hand, all right," David said.

The picture was still too blurry to make out the glimmer.

"Let's zoom in," Alex said, as he clicked on the target area with his mouse. "And sharpen," he said, pushing a few buttons on his keyboard. "There it is, guys. Any guesses about what it is?"

"It's a Wilson High School class ring," Sam said.

"I think you're right." David stared at the screen. He turned to Alex. "It's cool what you can do with all these manipulations."

"You can thank technology and eagle eyes over there," Alex said, pointing to Sam.

"Can we get a printout of this?" Joe asked.

A printer in the corner produced a color copy of what was on the screen in seconds. Joe looked at it quickly, then put it in his backpack. "Alex, that really helps us," Joe said. He looked at his watch. "We have a few minutes left before we have to leave, so could I ask for your professional opinion?"

"Semi-professional. I haven't graduated with my master's degree yet," Alex corrected him. "But I'll help you if I can."

"I've seen a few home videos, and this is a lot better quality. What do you think?" Joe said.

"Definitely not an amateur effort. If I graded it, it'd earn a B-plus, maybe an A. Your guy has studied filmmaking and also has access to some pretty nice equipment," Alex also answered.

"And I think the appearance of the ring is intentional," David said.

"You mean he *wants* it to be seen?" Sam said.

"Right," David said. "I don't think someone with film experience would get his hand in the way accidentally."

"Like the great mystery-and-horror-film director Alfred Hitchcock," Alex said. "He had a cameo role—just a brief walk-on part—in his films. Your culprit is proud of his work and puts a little piece of himself in it, too."

"Then he's probably a student here at the film school," David said.

Joe and Sam turned to look at him.

David explained his deduction. "If this guy is still wearing his high-school class ring, he probably recently graduated from high school. I've taken a few freshman and sophomore courses here at the college. I've noticed a few of these students wearing their high-school rings. I don't think juniors or seniors would." David saw Alex nodding his head in agreement. "Also, the college is one of the few places here in Oakdale with high-tech equipment. And, if the culprit has studied filmmaking, the college is the only place in the area that offers classes."

"Do you know who used the editing equipment Saturday?" Joe asked Alex, excitedly.

"Dr. Meacham keeps a list," he said. "But he's very private and probably won't let you see it." He stood up and walked to the door. "And while I wish I could help you even more, my time is up. I've got to get back to the grind. Dr. Meacham doesn't accept missed deadlines." He scribbled down a number on a sheet of paper and handed it to Joe. "Keep me posted on your investigation. And I'll keep an eye out around here to see who uses the equipment. If your vandal is getting back at the store, I don't think he'll stop with altering one tape."

Joe thanked Alex, and he and his friends headed out into the hall. The kids discussed Alex's last remark and agreed that the vandal might act against the store again. They also talked about their discoveries, which they spoke of excitedly.

Joe's mom said she would pick up Wishbone at the high school if they were running late. Joe decided he'd call his mom when he got to school. As they were walking down the hall, Joe paused at Dr. Meacham's office to thank him.

The door was slightly open. Joe was about to knock when he noticed something strange. The professor was watching a copy of the vandalized videotape. Joe saw the man rewind it and play it again. *He made a copy of it?* Joe wondered. That might be the tape Joe had seen on the professor's bookshelf, but it raised several questions: *What if the vandal is Dr. Meacham? Did he use the class ring to confuse us. What grudge would have against the video store?*

Chapter Six

When the last bell of the school day rang, Joe grabbed his backpack and started for the exit. He'd sat through hours of school with just one thing on his mind—showing Cassy the evidence he had discovered that morning. The Monday of classes had seemed to last forever.

Joe was almost outside when Sam came running up to him. She handed him a book. "You almost forgot your copy of *Phantom of the Opera*."

"Thanks, Sam." Joe put the book in his backpack. The assignment in their English class was to read the story during the holiday break. The plot sounded romantic, from what their teacher had said. That was *not* Joe's type of book. On the other hand, however, it was supposed to be a creepy tale, so Joe figured he might enjoy it.

When Joe arrived at the video store at four o'clock, Cassy was standing behind the counter staring at an open book in front of her. She looked a bit upset. But she also wore a red-felt Santa hat with a white, fuzzy ball on the tip. She looked up quickly, and before it registered who'd walked in, she said, "Hello. May I help you?"

Then Cassy realized it was Joe.

"Whew! I'm so glad you're here," she said.

As Joe set his backpack down, his heart was racing, as he looked at her. *Calm down, Joe,* he told himself. *There's no reason to be nervous.*

"How are you?" he asked.

"Stressed. I've got my diffy-Q final exam tomorrow. Yuck! And I've got to study. Would you mind if I went in the back so I could concentrate? You can always come get me if you need any help," she offered.

"Sure thing. . . . Diffy Q—that sounds hard," Joe said.

"Differential equations. Math. My major," she said. "And it's not hard—it's *impossible!*" She rubbed her eyes.

Cassy collected her things—a notebook, a textbook, and a jumbo-sized soft drink. "I know, I know, it's quite a beverage," she said, noticing how Joe eyed the big cup. "But I slept maybe only four hours last night, and I need the caffeine."

Joe felt disappointed as Cassy walked away. He'd raced to the video store to tell her about their discoveries, and to just talk to her. Now, just as quickly, she was disappearing into the back room.

Only a minute or so later, Cassy opened the door of the back room and called out to Joe, "If you ever have to study, or read, and it's slow around here, please do so. We're an education-friendly workplace."

Then she retreated into the back room.

But then she came out again. "Would you mind wearing this?" she asked. She took the red hat off her head and set it on the nearest shelf. "I want this place to get into the holiday spirit." Seeing Joe heading her way, she returned to study.

Joe walked over, picked up the hat, and placed it on his head. It fit tightly. The bigger problem would be if anyone he knew saw him in the hat. *All part of the job.*

After returning to the front counter, Joe pulled the video printout from his backpack.

Over a lunch of cheese nachos in the school cafeteria earlier that day, Joe, Sam, and David had tried to develop a profile of the culprit. They came up with two suspects—Ed and Dr. Meacham.

Joe reviewed all the evidence again. But he didn't get any further than he and his friends had that morning: The video vandal might have recently graduated from Wilson High School; probably attended the college's film school; used the school's video equipment; and wore a class ring. Adding everything up, it pointed to Ed.

But there was also Dr. Meacham. Both the professor and Ed had access to the equipment, and both may have owned Wilson High School class rings.

Suddenly, as if on cue, the entrance door opened and Ed walked in, a sour expression on his face.

"Nice hat," Ed said, as he looked around the store. "Wow! She really trusts you. Running the show all alone on only your third day of work."

Joe quickly hid the printout underneath the counter.

Looking at Joe, Ed said, "I'm sorry—did I interrupt you in the middle of something?"

"No. Look, I'm sorry about your losing the job." Joe extended his left hand. "Let's start over. I'm Joe Talbot."

The suspect looked a bit surprised, but he shook Joe's hand anyway. "Baines, Ed. And, like I said before, no big deal. I didn't even care about this job."

Joe saw a Wilson High School class ring glittering on Ed's finger. *It's him!* he thought.

"Okay, I said it was all right!" Ed shook Joe's hand loose. Joe had held onto Ed's hand for just a little too long, staring at the ring.

"Great." Joe tried to cover up his on-the-spot investigation. "I'm glad we got that out of the way. So do you want to rent a movie?"

Ed frowned.

Not a good way to try to start our friendship, Joe thought.

Ed handed Joe his employee shirt. "Give this to Cassy," he said. He ran his finger along the counter. "You know, I *do* want to rent a movie. How about *Fool's Gold*? Is that in?"

That's the movie that was sabotaged! Joe thought. *Could it be just a coincidence?*

Joe decided not to let Ed's odd request throw him off guard. He quickly tapped into the computer, acting as if he were checking on the movie's availability. "No, the two copies we have are out. Try back tomorrow."

Joe now realized that Ed at least was aware of the vandalism. Why else would he so smugly ask to rent such a little-known movie? But until Joe had absolute proof of Ed's guilt, he wasn't going to let him know what he knew.

Wanda and Wishbone walked in. Ed mumbled his thanks and walked around the counter and left quickly.

"Hello, Mr. Hollywood!" Wanda said. Seeing the hat on his head, she changed her greeting. "Hello, Mr. Holiday! I just came in to return this." She handed him the videotape she'd checked out the day before. "And I'm dropping off your pal."

As soon as she let go of Wishbone's leash, he ran around to the exit side of the store. The dog began to bark at Ed's retreating figure.

"Wishbone, stop!" Joe said. "Cassy is studying!"

But he was too late. Cassy came out from the storage room.

"Hi, everyone!" she said in a cheerful voice. Cassy was carrying her backpack.

"Oh, Cassy, I'm sorry about the noise," Joe apologized.

"Don't worry about it. Wishbone is quickly becoming my favorite dog." She bent down and nuzzled Wishbone's face. "Besides, I'm so tired of looking at numbers."

"Thanks for the compliment," Wishbone said. "But let's change the subject to something more edible."

Cassy began to rummage through her backpack. "I know it's in here somewhere," she said.

"Something for me? A snack? You shouldn't have. Really, Cassy. But, thank you," Wishbone said.

Then the terrier heard a jingling sound.

"What's that? Cookies don't jingle." He tilted his head to get a better angle on the sound.

Soon the awful truth revealed itself—it was no cookie, but a red dog collar decorated with jingle bells.

"Joe, can Wishbone wear this?" Cassy asked, as she headed toward the dog.

"Oh, sure. It'll look, uh . . . really cute on him," Joe responded, nodding his head.

"Cute?!? Since when have you ever described me as *'cute'?!?"* Wishbone could barely control himself.

"Oh, he'll look adorable," Wanda gushed. "Absolutely adorable."

"Joe, buddy, come to your senses! I can't wear this . . . *thing!"* Wishbone protested.

Cassy removed his collar and handed it to Joe. She put the red collar around his neck.

"Help me out, pal!"

But his friend just gave him a "what can I do?" look.

"What were you thinking, Joe? You can't let Cassy put this noisemaker on me!" Wishbone said. "But, then again, you're wearing a floppy, foot-long hat with a cotton ball hanging on the end. Maybe I should ask someone else for help."

Wishbone looked at the admiring faces in the circle

surrounding him—and realized he had no choice. He was stuck with the collar. *At least I don't have to wear a hat, too,* he told himself.

"He should wear that all year round," Wanda said. "It's adorable. You know, Cassy, you've got me in the spirit. I'm going to go home and finish putting up my decorations. And maybe I'll bake a fruit cake." She raised her eyebrows in anticipation.

"Sounds yummy," Wishbone said. "Save me a piece . . . or two, please."

As Wanda walked out, Stan and Margie Miller, the store's previous owners, walked in.

Wishbone didn't see who it was before running to greet the customers. *Ching! Ching!* His bells clanged as he raced around the counter.

"Yikes!" Wishbone screeched to a halt when he saw the

couple. "Gotta look smart. Can't have them bring up the subject of Ed again."

First Ed, and then his biggest supporters, Joe thought. But he said, "Hi! May I help you?"

They didn't answer. But fortunately, Stan and Margie—or at least Margie—appeared to be in a much happier mood than they had been the last time Joe had seen them.

Margie looked around the store, amazed. "You have done a great job with this store, Cassy. Look, honey!" Margie exclaimed to Stan. She pointed to an action-figure cardboard cutout that now stood in one corner. "Cassy, these are new!"

Margie's husband, however, hadn't gone much farther than the front door. As he looked around, he seemed sad and a little upset.

"Oh, Stan, I'm sorry," she said, as she went back to him.

Joe tried to make himself as close to invisible as possible. He didn't want to interrupt. He noticed that Cassy looked pretty uncomfortable, too.

"I'll wait out in the car," Stan said. He quickly walked around the counter to the exit door and left.

Joe and Cassy weren't quite sure what to say. Margie noticed Joe's wrinkled brow and Cassy's awkward fidgeting.

"Let me explain," she said. "Stan didn't really want to sell the store. But you know how hard it is to run this place—"

Cassy nodded in agreement.

"It was simply too much for us to run anymore. I talked Stan into selling. It was time for us to retire," Margie continued. "But Stan's still a little grumpy about that."

Margie reached down and patted Wishbone's head.

"Hey, fella, how are you?" Margie said playfully. "This terrier adds an especially nice touch here."

"I had no idea Mr. Miller was so upset about giving up the place. It must have been really difficult for him to help out me and my mom," Cassy said. "Please be sure and thank him again for us."

"Well, what can you do, right?" Margie said. "Besides, I'm not here to make you feel sorry for him. I'm here to rent a movie. Actually, it's a movie that Stan wants to see—*Fool's Gold*. Is it in?"

Joe and Cassy shared a look of surprise. "Uh . . . actually, no . . . our two copies are rented out right now," Cassy said.

Another odd coincidence? Joe thought. *Are the Millers suspects?*

"How'd you hear about that movie, by the way?" Cassy asked Margie. "I'm just curious, since it's not that popular."

Margie said, "Ed recommended it. He said that we'd love it."

Ed is trying to draw attention away from himself. He's creating other suspects, Joe thought. *Gotta give him points for thinking that up.*

"That Ed," Cassy said, shaking her head. "What a guy."

Chapter Seven

The ringing of Joe's alarm clock was not a welcome sound at seven-thirty on Tuesday morning. The night before, he'd begun reading *The Phantom of the Opera*. To his surprise, he hadn't been able to put the book down. It was turning out to be a very interesting mystery. The book had been published in 1911 by a French journalist named Gaston Leroux. He told the story through a narrator. He had created great characters: Christine, a beautiful opera singer haunted by memories of her late father; Raoul, a rich young man in love with her; and the Phantom. The Phantom haunted the elegant Paris Opera House, where Christine sang. Some thought he was just a figment of people's imaginations.

Joe had really plowed into the story. Reading it, he noticed that the plot was similar to his situation. New managers had taken over the opera house, the same thing that had happened at the video store. The new personnel wouldn't fulfill the Phantom's demands the way the former management had. This seemed very similar to what had happened with Ed—while Stan and Margie seemed to give him a lot of freedom, Cassy didn't put up with his independent ways.

As the story progressed, the Phantom started to pull pranks. And, like the mystery person who had videotaped David, the Phantom managed to creep around the large theater without ever being seen by anyone.

The new managers at the opera house suspected the pranks were all part of a hoax, a joke on the new staff. However, in Joe's situation, he suspected the vandalism at the video store was not a prank. Reading the book made him even more eager to solve the real-life mystery. Besides, the idea of someone lurking around and secretly videotaping one of his friends gave him the creeps. And Joe was enjoying his new job. He wanted to put an end to the prank so Cassy could be happy and enjoy her job.

Joe was trying to figure out how he felt about Cassy. He knew that he really liked being around her. And she seemed to enjoy talking to him and having his company. But his job at the video store was not going to last forever, and he hoped they could become friends outside of the workplace, too.

Joe found himself getting more and more confident around Cassy lately. *And if I can solve this mystery, she'll really be impressed.*

He finally got out of bed. Today was the last day of school before Christmas vacation began. After three P.M., he'd be able to devote two full weeks to working at the video store. He washed and dressed in record time and ran downstairs. His mom left a message on the breakfast-room table. She had an early-morning dental appointment.

"Good morning, Wishbone!" Joe said, as he reached for a breakfast bar.

The dog watched Joe put on his jacket, grab his books and backpack, then head for the door.

Joe stopped and turned to his pal. "I'll come get you right after school, before I go off to work," he said. "I'll see you then. Oh . . . and don't forget—you can only eat one cookie today."

"Oh, cookies are only the second thing on my mind," Wishbone answered. "And about that one-cookie-a-day limit: I'm currently negotiating with Ellen on that deal. I feel good about how it's going, so you might want to stock up. I'll let you know." But Joe was already out the door.

"It's time to get down to business," Wishbone said. "*Show* business."

He'd almost made a Hollywood connection in Oakdale the day before. So instead of making plans to go to Hollywood, he decided not to give up on his hometown. He would continue to search. Maybe he'd find someone who was really famous, someone who would recognize his star potential. *And from there, who knows? A talk show? A TV pilot? A movie?*

Wishbone used a nearby plant as a stand-in for a live audience. "Today, on *Wishbone Live,* we're talking about how to convince your human pals that one walk a day just isn't enough. We'll also have our segment called 'Squeaky Toys— Where You Can Get the Best Bargains,' plus a quick and easy recipe for great-tasting biscuits," he said.

Wishbone thought about that particular scenario for a few moments.

"Nah," Wishbone said. "I need more of an adventure."

He skidded dramatically along the hardwood floor into the living room.

"In this week's episode," the terrier went on, "Wishbone rescues a runaway speeding train, using only his bare paws and his shrewd mind. . . . Well, I'm on the right track," the dog noted, "but I need a larger screen."

He ran back into the hallway and up the stairs.

"They said it couldn't be done. But he refused to believe them. Against all odds, Wishbone must save the world."

He perched on the highest step and practiced his pose for the life-sized cardboard cutout poster of him that Cassy would proudly display at the store.

"That's it! A perfect story for my first feature film! I've got to spread the word!"

Wishbone ran down the stairs and out his doggie door into the backyard. He zoomed around the house with only one thing on his mind. He'd even forgotten to grab a cookie before he left.

As he made his way down Forest Lane, Wishbone noticed an unusual face in his neighborhood. "Hey!" he said to the person. "Welcome to the— Oh . . . it's . . . it's . . . but it can't be!" Wishbone thought he recognized the Hollywood-type guy, even though he was far away. "Jim O'Leary—I *love* your movies! In fact, we watched one just the other night!" the dog called out to him. Joe had rented one of the star's movies on Friday. "I laughed and laughed and laughed." He was exaggerating a *little* bit, but it probably wouldn't hurt. The terrier made his way across the street.

Think about something funny . . . something funny . . . something . . . Wishbone thought.

The man looked at Wishbone. The terrier cleared his throat, determined to say something hilarious.

"Hey, I know you!" the man said to the dog. "What are you doing out of your yard—and without a leash?"

Oh, it's just the cable guy, Wishbone thought, as he breathed a sigh of disappointment.

Chapter Eight

After school Joe had stopped by his house and picked up Wishbone. When they arrived at the store at four o'clock, he told Cassy about what had happened yesterday at Oakdale College and at the store with Ed.

"I don't know what surprises me more," Cassy said. "Your detective skills, or Ed's ability to do something so sneaky."

Joe tried not to smile at Cassy's compliment. He felt his Santa hat slipping and adjusted it.

"Ed ran this store by himself for almost a week!" she said. "Do you know what he could have done in that time? I'm really counting on this place to be a big success. My mother needs it to succeed, and she's already so stressed—" Cassy caught herself and looked at Joe.

I wonder what problems Cassy and her mom are having, Joe thought. He still hadn't learned any more about Miss Bennett than the little he'd been told days ago. He didn't want to ask Cassy, though. She didn't seem to want to talk about it.

Cassy went on. "Ed could have ruined our business. Actually, he still might. Who knows if he'll strike again? . . . You know, the more I think about it, suppose Ed isn't the culprit. It *could* be a coincidence that he wears a Wilson High class ring, that he's studying filmmaking, and that he's interested in *Fool's Gold,* the sabotaged title. It's unlikely, but it still could be a bizarre coincidence of events."

Just like in The Phantom of the Opera, Joe thought. *The narrator thinks the Phantom exists, even though there is no hard evidence to prove it, but others don't believe in his existence. And I'm convinced Ed is the culprit, even if others doubt it.*

Joe couldn't keep quiet any longer. "Cassy, it can't be anybody *but* Ed. All the evidence you just mentioned, plus his access to high-tech video equipment, point to him." His voice shook a little bit. He'd never talked to Cassy like that, nor had he ever disagreed with her. She was, after all, his boss.

"Okay, okay, you're right," she said. "It's hard to admit that he could be a criminal. And now I've got to figure out what I'm going to do with this information. Let's get back to work, maybe earn some money to pay for the replacement copy of *Fool's Gold.* I'll have to think for a while about how I'm going to handle this."

Cassy paused for a few seconds.

"You like your job, don't you?" she asked Joe suddenly.

Joe wasn't sure where this line of questioning was going, but he nodded. "Sure, it's great," he said.

"It's not shooting three-pointers at Madison Square Garden, but it's fun, right?" she asked.

"Sure," he said, playing along.

"Here's the un-fun part. Remember yesterday, when I printed out the overdue-video report?" she asked.

Joe nodded again. The computer could print out just about anything with a few commands and the touch of a couple of keys. It was possible to check on all the accounts that were currently renting a tape, conduct a store inventory, and make a list of everyone who owed late fees or had a video overdue.

"Well," Cassy said, "today you get to call the delinquent accounts. It's just to tell the renters about their late fee or overdue video. Most people appreciate the reminder. But just as a warning—sometimes people aren't too happy to hear from the store. Don't take it personally. Be polite, like you always are. If anyone gets too rude, find a way to get off the phone."

After that introduction to his assignment, Joe hoped the list was pretty short.

"I'll be working on a stack of paperwork in the office. Trust me—you'd rather be making these calls than doing what I have to do," she said. She got on one knee and looked at Wishbone. "I'll see you in a little while, buddy. Keep Joe company while I'm gone," she said, and she nuzzled the terrier's face. Cassy got up and walked toward the back of the store.

Lucky dog, Joe thought. *Always getting all the attention.*

He got to work and printed out the report. It numbered fifteen names. Scanning through the list, Joe recognized a few people. One was Coach Roberts, his basketball coach. He had out an overdue yoga tape.

Joe smiled at the idea of the tall, muscular man stretching and relaxing, with a content look on his face. But the coach just didn't strike Joe as being the type to do yoga.

Then Joe felt a little funny as the image of the yoga-exercising coach stuck in his mind. His job gave him an unusual opportunity. He could find out what movies everyone in Oakdale rented. He could peek into people's private lives. *Coach Roberts might not want anyone to know he does yoga.* Joe decided that he would keep these kinds of discoveries to himself.

Ironically, when Joe looked down at the list, the name "Ed Baines" jumped out at him from the paper. Joe didn't want to call him about an overdue video. He wanted to bust him for vandalizing the expensive tape and making David look foolish. *But it's Cassy's decision, not mine,* he told himself.

Calling Ed about a late fee wasn't going to be a pleasant experience, Joe knew. *Maybe there are two Ed Baineses in this town,* he thought. But he knew there wasn't a good chance of that.

You've done a few things harder than this, Joe told himself. But that didn't make picking up the phone any easier. *Besides, what are you going to tell Cassy—that you chickened out and couldn't call Ed?*

Joe figured he'd get this call over with first. Picking up the receiver and dialing the number, he hoped Ed wouldn't be home.

"Baines residence," a young-sounding boy answered.

"Hi," Joe said. "May I speak to Ed, please?"

"He's at work. This is his brother, Mark," he replied.

Gosh! Ed sure found another job fast, Joe thought. *Well, at least I can just leave him a message and not have to talk to him.*

"I'm calling from The Movie Shoppe. Would you mind telling your brother that the tape he rented from our store is overdue?" Joe asked.

"You should be able to tell him yourself," the boy said. "That's where Ed's working."

Joe gulped. *So his brother doesn't know he was fired,* he thought. *This assignment isn't going to be easy, after all.* Should he lie for Ed? He had to decide quickly. "Actually, Ed's not working here any longer," Joe said. *What else can I say?* Joe told himself. *I can't lie for him.* But he didn't have to tell the boy Ed was fired, either.

"Whoa! Wait till I tell Mom. Ed's going to be in a lot of trouble," Mark said gleefully.

"Would you also please tell him that his rental video is overdue?" Joe asked.

"Sure, I'll tell him," Mark said. "'Bye."

That didn't go well at all, Joe thought. He looked back at his list and dialed the next number. *I can't imagine any of these calls being anywhere near as difficult as that one.*

Joe was right. He zoomed through the rest of his phone calls. When Cassy returned to the counter, Joe was checking in some tapes. He and Wishbone had even helped a couple of customers.

"Are you already done with calling the customers?" Cassy asked.

Joe nodded.

"Wow! That was really quick," she said. "Was it painless, too?"

Joe explained how he had to call the Baines household, and how he handled the situation.

"Bravo!" Cassy said. "I doubt I would have dealt with it that well. I'm so angry at Ed right now I could scream."

"You sure have enough reason to be angry," Joe said.

"I've decided not to get myself needlessly upset, however," Cassy said. "I'm calling the authorities to report the vandalized tape. I probably should have called them last Sunday, when we received it."

She pulled a phone book out from beneath the counter. She looked up the number of the police department, then dialed the phone.

She put her hand over the mouthpiece and turned to Joe. "Ed's not going to get away with this," she said. Joe figured that the phone must have been picked up at the police department because Cassy removed her hand from the mouthpiece and said, "Hello. I need to report a crime, please."

Cassy spoke for several minutes, then hung up, a triumphant look on her face.

"They're sending over an officer immediately," she announced.

76

"I'll be on the lookout," Wishbone said, as he sat at the window. He expected to see flashing lights and sirens, but nothing like that happened. Wishbone recognized Officer Krulla. He parked in front of the store in his familiar squad car.

The officer got out of his car and came into the shop. "Hi, Joe, hi, Wishbone," the policeman said.

Joe had aided the police department in the past. He had been on an overnight stakeout of the local library with Officer Krulla about three years ago. The two had worked together a few times since.

"Good afternoon, Officer Krulla!" Wishbone said. "Ed did it."

"You must be Cassy Bennett," Krulla said upon seeing the girl. He shook her hand. "You reported some kind of video vandalism involving David Barnes."

As Cassy and Joe explained the entire scenario, Officer Krulla took notes on his official pad.

"This is a new one for me," he admitted. "What a strange crime. Are you sure it wasn't an accident? Imagine someone just taping their kid at college, and the camera somehow zooms in on David. And the person accidentally tapes it over this movie. It is nothing malicious, just a coincidence."

"Oh, no, no coincidence," Wishbone said.

Officer Krulla paused. "You know, having heard myself say it, that seems pretty unlikely. How could someone take Dr. Meacham's videocassette, tape over it with David on it, and return it to the professor—all accidentally? But why would anyone want to hurt any of you?"

"I know! We're so nice," Wishbone said.

"I don't know," Cassy said. "But the tape, according to our store records, has been legally in the possession of only two people—Dr. Meacham and me. I can't believe—well, I know *I* didn't do it. And the professor? I just don't think so."

"You never know, Cassy." Then Wishbone said to Officer Krulla, "He's not tempted by candy. That is never a good sign."

"Excuse me," a voice interrupted. A young boy stood at the counter by the entrance door.

"Where'd you come from?" Wishbone asked. "I didn't even know you were in here. I wonder why I missed your scent. I'm supposed to keep track of who comes in here. And I see you don't have any candy to go along with the movie you are holding. Have you checked out the new display? Be a sport. How about buying something off the rack?"

"Would you like to rent that?" Joe asked the young boy, referring to the movie he was holding.

"Oh, no. I'm returning it—but it has a problem. I mean, a defect. A . . . problem," he said nervously.

Joe took the video from the boy. He pulled the tape out of its plastic case. He recognized the title, and he knew the store had paid a lot for it. "What's wrong with it?" Joe asked the boy.

"Just watch it and you'll see," the boy said.

Joe put the tape in the VCR at the counter and pushed Play. The regular movie played for about ten seconds. Then the screen dissolved to a solid blue color for a few seconds. Next came some tape showing an Oakdale police car.

It's the vandal! Wishbone immediately recognized the high-quality handiwork.

Whoever was shooting the videotape took a second to look at his or her watch. The person's wrist could be seen at the side of the screen. The time on the watch read 7:45.

Aha—a clue! Where have I seen that watch?. . . It looks so familiar, Wishbone thought.

The car was parked on the campus of Oakdale College. Then came the same kind of close-up, zoom-in shot that had been on the earlier vandalized video.

The phantom strikes again! But who will be the victim this time? Wishbone thought.

Officer Krulla looked nervous. "Hey . . . that's—that's . . ." he said. Then he fell silent.

The video camera had focused directly on Officer Krulla himself. He sat in his car keeping a watchful eye on the college campus. The tape continued to play as he pulled over a small box from the seat next to him.

This is suspenseful. What could be in it? Wishbone thought. He began to run through a list of imagined possibilities in his head.

The young boy couldn't hold back a snicker when Officer Krulla pulled out a jelly-filled doughnut on-screen.

The policeman on the screen took a big bite. The gooey jelly squirted out the opposite end, plopping onto his uniform. Then the officer finished that doughnut and took out another from the box. And another . . . Soon he had emptied the whole box, and chocolate, jelly, glaze, and sprinkles covered his uniform. The scene ended with the policeman reclining his seat back. He closed his eyes and patted his stomach contentedly. Then, only seconds later, the regular part of the movie picked up on-screen.

Standing dead-silent at the counter in the video store, Officer Krulla looked humiliated. His face was red, and his eyes were wide as saucers.

Joe and Cassy tried not to smile. She patted Officer Krulla's shoulder gently, sympathetically.

"Thanks, Cassy," Krulla said. Then he became angry. "That was yesterday morning, about seven-thirty. I had just

gotten off the night shift. Each of us officers has to work it once a week. It was a long, ten-hour shift. I had bought myself a snack. There is nothing wrong with a doughnut . . . or two," he said.

"You can say that again," Wishbone said.

"This secret videotaping has gone too far!" Cassy said angrily, shaking her head. "And now still another one of our most expensive videos has been butchered!"

"We have another clue," Joe said. "The wristwatch. But it's a very common brand. I have one just like it, and I noticed you also have one, Officer Krulla."

"Whew! That was close, Joe," Wishbone said. "You were almost a suspect."

The dog looked up at the kid. "You know, you look familiar," he said. No one but Wishbone was paying any attention to the kid. But the boy didn't seem bothered by that. Instead, he looked as if he was enjoying watching the reactions of those around him to the surprise film clip they had just viewed.

"Now we're going to mount an all-out search to find this vandal," said Krulla, the latest victim of the video scam. "It's personal," he mumbled.

"Cassy, Cassy, over here!" Wishbone reminded her. "We've got an unhappy customer waiting."

Cassy turned to the boy. "I'm sorry about that tape. Let me get you another copy. I'm sure we have one," Cassy said. "What name is this account under?"

"Baines," he announced. "Ed Baines. I'm his brother, Mark. Joe just called me before to say the tape was overdue."

"Mark, explain what you know about this tape," Officer Krulla said.

This is certainly an interesting development, Wishbone thought.

Chapter Nine

Officer Krulla stood rigid and red-faced at the bench outside Dr. Meacham's office at Oakdale College. Officer Krulla had decided to question Dr. Meacham about Ed. Since Ed was a film student at the college, Dr. Meacham probably knew him. The policeman called the professor, and he agreed to see him on campus at a quarter to six. Joe and Cassy asked to come along. Officer Krulla had agreed. "There goes that theory," he said. "There's no chance Ed's our video vandal."

Cassy and Joe looked up from their seats. "Why? What did he say?" Joe asked.

"Let's not discuss it here," the policeman suggested.

Joe, Cassy, and Wishbone followed the officer to a small nook at the end of the hallway where they could talk without being overheard by passing students and faculty.

"So, what did the professor say?" Cassy asked.

Officer Krulla sighed. "Ed has an airtight alibi. The best I've ever heard, in fact," the policeman said. "The entire time David was at work at the college, including when he was filmed," he said, "Ed was nearby in the film school's library. He works there part-time, filing tapes and doing other technical duties. Professor Meacham's security camera actually taped it all. He was worried about department security, so he installed a video camera with a time code to monitor the library. The tape shows Ed working there the whole time. He doesn't leave the frame for more than a few seconds. He couldn't have a more perfect alibi."

"How ironic," Cassy commented. "He's proven innocent of videotaping by reason of being videotaped."

"We'll just have to look for other suspects," Officer Krulla said.

Joe remembered that the narrator from Leroux's *The Phantom of the Opera* believed that the Phantom existed, even though others did not. "But *I know* that Ed is guilty," Joe said.

"But, Joe, he can't be! How could Ed be at the film school's library during the exact same time David was videotaped?" Cassy argued.

Joe couldn't answer that question.

"Son, I admire your persistence. But Cassy's right—it can't be Ed," the policeman said. "Let's consider other suspects. Who else would have a reason to hurt your business, Cassy?"

The question surprised her. "My mom and I have only had the store for two weeks. I know a lot of people here at school, but I'm sure none of them would want to hurt me. And then we also have our regular customers at the store," she said. "But why would they want to hurt us?" She paused for a moment. "But, you know, now that I think of it, there is one other person—ooh, I don't even want to think about it."

"You're not saying they did it, you're just considering it," Officer Krulla assured her.

Cassy looked at Joe. He was sure he knew what she was thinking.

"Stan Miller," Joe said, exchanging looks with Cassy.

83

"He didn't want to sell the place, but his wife, Margie, talked him into it. He came into the store once and got so upset that he had to leave."

Cassy nodded her head in agreement. "Now that I think about it, I was on campus at seven-thirty the day David was taped. I saw Mr. Miller walk by that morning carrying a big black bag. It could have held a video camera," she said.

"And I know he's lived in Oakdale his entire life and gone to all its schools, so maybe he owns a Wilson High class ring," Officer Krulla said.

"Cassy, did Stan Miller see you? If he did, did he seem surprised?" Officer Krulla asked.

"He saw me, but he wasn't surprised. He knows I'm a student at the college. He waved and then he turned around quickly and walked in the opposite direction. But that could be because he's upset about the store," she suggested.

"Anyone else you suspect?" Officer Krulla asked.

"Other than Stan Miller . . . If Mr. Miller holds a grudge about selling the store, it should be against his wife. She talked him into selling. Does this make sense?"

"I see your point. Any other suspects?" the policeman said.

Joe thought about the two people they had just discussed. A third person could not be omitted from the list of suspects—Dr. Meacham.

Joe told Officer Krulla and Cassy about the accidental discovery yesterday morning. "The tape was labeled December 18—the day David was taped," he said. "And then I later saw the professor watching it. I don't know what that means, but—"

"I didn't notice if he wore a watch like the one in the tape," Officer Krulla said.

"Even if he does, so do you and I," Joe said, pointing to his wrist. "Lots of people do."

"Gosh," Cassy said with a sigh. "It's hard to think of people as suspects."

"Let's go at this from a new angle," Joe suggested. "Alex, Dr. Meacham's assistant, said the culprit uses high-tech equipment. That's not available on every street corner in Oakdale. We need a list of who had access to the film department's equipment."

Joe still thought Ed was their chief suspect, but he knew that it would not hurt to check out other possible leads. "Dr. Meacham keeps a list," Joe explained. "A log of everyone who uses the college's editing equipment. Alex said he is private about the list and would not let us see it." Joe turned to Officer Krulla. "But maybe if you asked, he'd let you see it."

Officer Krulla shook his head. "Dr. Meacham was not only annoyed, but upset, that I'd asked him about Ed. He added that he'd expect a search warrant if I wanted to examine anything in the department," the officer explained.

"Why is he being so difficult?" Cassy asked. "It's such a tiny issue to ask to look at his list. These aren't the Roswell files, after all."

"It's as though he doesn't want us to solve this crime," Joe said.

"We've found suspect number three," Officer Krulla announced. "Congratulations. We've got quite a roster." He patted Joe on the back. "I'm needed back at the station-house, and you need to get to your homes. It's almost six o'clock. I'll keep my eyes op——" He stopped suddenly and looked down the hallway. "Did anybody else see that?"

Joe and Cassy also looked down the hallway, but they saw nothing unusual.

"No. What was it?" Cassy asked.

"I think I saw the Baines kid. But it couldn't be. Why would he follow us here?" Officer Krulla said.

"Ed is a student here. Maybe he has an evening class," Joe said.

"No. I mean the little one—Mark," Officer Krulla said.

Cassy looked skeptical. "No, I don't think so," she said, shaking her head. "He'd have to have followed us here."

"Stranger things have happened recently," Officer Krulla said. "For instance, how did the culprit get his—or her—hands on Dr. Meacham's and the Baineses' tapes?"

"Good question," Joe said. "And I've got an idea about how it's being done." He thought of a way to prove Ed's guilt—and to bring himself closer to Cassy. "Let's stake out the store tonight."

"It's worked before," Officer Krulla said.

"You two have done this before?" Cassy asked.

"A few years ago," Joe answered. "We had a similar situation occur in the public library. We staked out the place and found out who was behind it. And then there was some trouble at the bookstore when I worked there last summer. If our guy gets his hands on the tapes somehow, maybe he's breaking in and sneaking them out at night."

It might just be me and Cassy, Joe thought. He felt happy and alarmed at the same time.

"You know, Ed never returned his key," Cassy said. "Even though the security videotapes in the film library support Ed's innocence, maybe, just maybe, he figured a way to get around that. Maybe he is the vandal."

"At tonight's stakeout, I don't think we'll run into any danger. But I'll have to check with your mom, Joe. Cassy, since you are no longer a minor, it's your decision. I'll check with my boss to make sure involving civilians in a stakeout is not breaking any police regulations," Officer Krulla said. "And maybe I'll bring doughnuts." He smiled.

Okay, so it'll be me, Cassy, and Officer Krulla, Joe thought. *And Wishbone. Speaking of Wishbone, where is my dog?*

Wishbone stood in front of the college administration building. He'd sneaked away from the group when he saw Ed's little brother. He was following him and didn't want to blow his cover.

But when he turned the corner, he found the college to be a little more crowded than he'd expected. Classes had just let out, and people swarmed the sidewalk.

Wow! The college didn't seem quite so big last time, Wishbone thought.

He looked around. It was final-exam time, four days before Christmas. Students and teachers mobbed the campus even at six o'clock. Backpacks and sneakers surrounded him. It was noisy, full of laughter and talking. Other students sat around reading. And the birds and squirrels were too numerous to count. *My kind of place,* Wishbone thought. *Too bad I don't have enough time to enjoy it!*

"Excuse me, pardon me. Oops, excuse me," Wishbone said, as he wiggled his way out of the crowd. "Clear a path, please! Coming through!"

Change of strategy. Wishbone dodged another pair of legs as he went up the front steps of the building. Even from his superior vantage point, he'd lost Mark.

"Rats!" he said, sitting on the step. "Oh, well. I've gotta be able to think on my paws."

"Hey, cutie!" a girl said, kneeling down beside Wishbone. "What are you doing here?" She handed him a piece of a bagel she was eating.

"Why, thank you. You wouldn't happen to have seen—" he began.

But the girl had already walked away.

"Oh, my gosh! Is that Jason LeForge—the world's greatest spy?" Wishbone could not be mistaken this time. This was truly a Hollywood type. "Well, greatest actor who *plays* a spy! Jason! Wait for me!" Wishbone saw the man across the walk. He bounded down the steps. In a single leap, he was on the ground running.

His feat drew the attention of a few kids. They pointed at him as he ran. *Already drawing fans, I see,* the dog thought. *Now, if I can just get LeForge to notice me!*

He slipped into the revolving door LeForge had entered. Pushing the door with his nose, he made his way into the building. Wishbone realized it must be the student union. It was huge, with a small store, information desk, and cafeteria. A clear path ahead of him, he ran full speed ahead.

And then he heard those dreaded words—"Hey! Dogs aren't allowed in here!"

"How can the halls of higher education be closed to the noble dog?" Wishbone protested. "Besides, I've got a mission to accomplish."

But he knew not to stick around for the answer. He

darted behind a group of students. Peeking out, he made sure he'd lost the security guard who was now on his trail.

"And here I go," Wishbone said.

He slipped into the small store. Pencils, paper, a small candy counter—but no LeForge. *His reputation precedes him— he is master of disguise,* Wishbone thought. *He must have learned something doing all those films.*

Out in the entryway again, he saw the security guard's head looking out over the crowd. "Try to fit in, try to fit in," Wishbone reminded himself. But finding this difficult to do, he settled for a quick sneak.

He made his way down a hall. A cafeteria proved hard to look over, and hard to resist. Wishbone walked in. But then he saw Dr. Meacham coming toward him. In addition to a book bag, the professor carried a tray with a hamburger and fries.

"Dinnertime, is it?" Wishbone asked. "I suppose you wouldn't care to share, would you?"

Then, suddenly, the professor caught Wishbone's eye.

Dr. Meacham pointed his finger at the dog, dropping his tray. Fries flew everywhere, and the professor's drink splashed onto a girl sitting near him.

"A dog is in the cafeteria! Where's security?" the professor said in a loud voice.

"Ahhh!" Wishbone said in an even louder voice. He turned and bolted out of the cafeteria. He heard the security guard's footsteps moving fast behind him. But he dodged down another hall and managed to evade him again.

Wishbone panted and tried to catch his breath.

"You'd think the professor had seen a cat or something!" he said. "And I didn't even get a fry!"

He looked up after a few seconds, ready to return to Joe and get back home and enjoy dinner himself. *Espionage is exhausting work,* he thought.

Looking up, he couldn't believe what he saw. To the left, Mark Baines. To the right, LeForge. And they both were only a few feet away. *Stardom or sleuthing? Celebrity or crime patrol?*

"Hollywood will have to wait!" Wishbone said, as he ran after Mark. But his chase was short. Two turns around corners and he realized he'd lost Mark again.

"Ouch!" Wishbone said. "I need to work on my secret agent skills." He sat down to think for a minute.

And Jason LeForge walked by—or a guy who looked a whole lot like LeForge. But alas, it was not him.

Rats! It's Double-O-Nobody. My plans have been foiled again, Wishbone thought.

Chapter Ten

"Oooh! A stakeout. Sounds like fun," Wanda said, as she sat on the couch next to Ellen. "Mind if I come along? What time, and where?"

"Only if you bring that fruitcake you made," Wishbone said. He sat in his favorite red chair in the Talbot study.

Joe was sitting on a chair next to the terrier. He reached over to pat Wishbone, and the dog noticed his long face.

"Sure, Miss Gilmore." Joe tried to sound upbeat. "It's tonight, and we're meeting at the video store at seven-thirty."

"Oh, drats!" she said. "Tonight I have pottery class. Afterward, I always go out for coffee with the girls. I don't think I can make it."

"Well, can the cake still come?" Wishbone asked.

"Too bad," Joe said, trying not to smile.

"I told Officer Krulla it would be all right for you to go, after he reassured me you would be in no danger. Be careful tonight, Joe," Ellen said.

"I will, Mom," Joe said.

"Sam and David are going to be there tonight, right?" Wanda asked.

"No, just Cassy, Officer Krulla, and me," Joe explained. "Just the video store staff and a policeman."

"And me! Don't forget about me!" Wishbone said. "Or did you include me in 'staff'?"

"Three people should be enough," Wanda said, nudging Ellen. "Wouldn't want *too* many people there."

Aha! Wishbone thought, catching the looks Wanda and Ellen were giving Joe. *Now I get it. Joe wants to be alone with Cassy—well, alone with Cassy, me, and Officer Krulla—tonight.*

Ellen nodded her head. "Right. Too many people *might* throw off the crook," she agreed.

This could get embarrassing, Wishbone thought. *I've got to get Joe out of here.* The dog walked to the stairs, hoping Joe would follow.

"I've got to get a few things together before I leave. I don't know if I'll be home tonight, but I will be in by morning. It's winter break, so I don't have to worry about missing classes," Joe said. "Officer Krulla will be with us. I'll be okay." Joe stood up and walked toward Wishbone. "I think I'll go change clothes."

"Clothes," Wishbone said. "All that worry about what you're going to wear makes me glad to be me."

"What's wrong with what you have on? It looks—Oh," Ellen said.

"Ellen, Ellen! Psst! Over here! You're embarrassing Joe," Wishbone whispered.

She raised her eyebrows, and Wishbone knew she understood. "Change clothes, right," she said, smiling at Wanda.

"Joe, let's get out of here—while you still have some dignity left," Wishbone said.

92

Wow! That was uncomfortable, Joe thought. He figured it was a good time to get out before it got worse.

He ran up the stairs and put on a sweatshirt. He grabbed his backpack and put a few things inside, including *The Phantom of the Opera,* though he hoped he wouldn't have time to read it. He looked around his room. Joe got his sleeping bag and pillow. The night was really cold, and he needed padding for the hard floor in the video store.

"C'mon, Wishbone! See ya, Mom! 'Bye, Miss Gilmore!" Joe said as he came back downstairs, got his jacket, and ran out the door.

As Joe and Wishbone walked to the video store, Joe felt nervous. *What if we don't catch him tonight?* he thought. *What, then? The store's future—and mine with Cassy—might depend on the next few hours.*

He tried to shake the thought out of his head, but he couldn't. *Maybe if Officer Krulla's not there yet,* he thought, *I could ask Cassy to go see a movie. Just to get together outside of our job.*

He didn't want to call it a date, but that was what he hoped for. When he had first met her, he didn't even consider it a possibility. She was so cool. She seemed to enjoy being with him, and they had a few things in common.

He was still unsure about their age difference. *Would a college student date a freshman in high school?* Maybe Cassy wouldn't care, since she thought he looked and acted older than he was.

Joe's confidence soared. It was time to take a chance. He promised himself that he would ask Cassy out that night. Hoping that he'd have a few minutes alone with Cassy, before Officer Krulla arrived, he picked up his pace.

Unfortunately, they found the policeman waiting at the video store's front door. Officer Krulla was still in uniform. He carried a canvas bag and a sleeping bag. "Hi," he said. "Ready for an exciting night?"

93

I was, Joe thought. But he remembered he was there to catch a crook, too. "Yes, I'm ready," he said.

Cassy arrived and unlocked the front door. "Let's get this started!" she said, letting them into the store. "Hey, you!" Cassy looked at Joe and gave him a big smile. "This is really a great idea."

She'll say yes, he thought. *Now I've just got to get a minute alone with her.*

"Wow!" Officer Krulla whistled. Cassy had set out food on the short front counter. Popcorn, chips, a pizza, some cookies—it looked like a party more than a stakeout.

"I'd figured we'd hide out down here," she explained. She went behind the long front counter. She had a sleeping bag, several pillows, and blankets on the floor. "And we'd need snacks to keep our energy up. I've turned off the alarm by the exit door. We don't want to set it off accidentally."

"Great idea," Joe said.

"And," Cassy said, "I thought it might make it a little easier to tell you guys."

"Tell us what?" Joe asked.

"The bad news," she said. "If another tape gets vandal-ized, we might have to close the store."

Joe's face fell. "Why?" he asked.

"Joe, I'm sorry. But my mom—this job was supposed to be relaxing for her. But it's so stressful. She's worried about me getting hurt. She's worried that whoever is doing this may do more to the store than just tape over our movies. Word will get around Oakdale that a vandal is striking our store and we may lose business. Should I go on? And if it happens again, I think she might decide it's not worth it," she explained.

"Cassy, I've never met your mom," Officer Krulla said. "When does she come into the store?"

"Well, actually," Cassy said, looking at the floor, "she

hasn't come in lately. She's still finishing up some business out of state. But I talk to her pretty often and keep her updated."

"So, where is she? Does she own another video store somewhere?" Officer Krulla asked.

"She's in California, and she does not own another video store," Cassy said firmly.

Joe still couldn't figure out why Cassy wouldn't say anything about her mom. *What's the mystery?* he wondered. Miss Bennett was the only subject Cassy acted funny about.

"I'd like to meet her when she returns," the policeman said.

Cassy grabbed a cookie off the counter. "Hey, Wishbone. You hungry?"

There she goes again, Joe thought. *We start talking about her mom, and Cassy changes the subject.*

Wishbone ran up to her and took a chunk out of the cookie.

"It's dark outside," Joe reminded them. "Let's sit on the floor."

The three arranged their sleeping bags on the floor. They propped pillows against the cabinet doors. Joe and Cassy sat down. Officer Krulla did, too. With a little effort, he sat cross-legged on the floor—but not before he moved all the snacks down. The terrier plopped down in the middle of the group and yawned. He'd had an action-packed day.

Cassy looked at him and yawned, too. "It's going to be a long night, guys," she said. "I wish we could watch a movie."

"Why can't we?" Officer Krulla said. He seemed like a kid in a candy store as he looked up at all the movies behind the counter.

"The glow of the screen and the sound might throw off Ed—I mean whoever," Joe said. "We can't have the store look any different than it does normally, when it's closed."

"Maybe we shouldn't even talk. Our voices could carry through the glass and outside the store," Cassy said.

They agreed. The group sat in an uncomfortable silence. Officer Krulla began to hum. Then he remembered their vow of silence and he stopped. Joe looked around anxiously at first, but then he eventually relaxed. Cassy scratched Wishbone behind the ears.

"Wow!" she said, whispering. "Wishbone might be able to stay like this forever, but I am *bored*. I'm going to fall asleep. Isn't there anything that we can do to entertain ourselves?" she asked.

"We could play cards," Officer Krulla whispered.

"Anybody got any cards?" Cassy asked.

"Not me," Joe said.

"Me, either," Cassy said.

"Don't look at me," the policeman said. "I was hoping one of you might have a deck of cards."

"Books, anyone?" Cassy suggested. "I have an organic chemistry textbook. We could turn this into an educational experience."

Joe remembered that he had brought *The Phantom of the Opera* with him. He pulled it out of his backpack. "I have this," he offered.

"Oh, great!" Cassy said, and she almost clapped her hands. "A scary book to read in the dark." She looked outside at the streetlight that threw a few beams of light into the store. "Well, almost dark," she said.

Officer Krulla took out a flashlight from his canvas bag. "I think we can turn this small light on," he said.

Cassy pulled the popcorn close to her. "Okay, Joe, you start," she said. She smiled when she saw Wishbone locate a few pieces of popcorn. Then he returned to his spot and closed his eyes.

"I'll just read it quietly," Joe said.

"Page one," he began. "'The Opera ghost really existed. He was not, as was long believed, a creature of the imagination of the artists, the superstition of the managers, or a product of the absurd and impressionable brains—'"

Officer Krulla interrupted him. "What was that noise?" he said, suddenly alert. "Did anybody else hear that?"

"Somebody just turned in a video," Cassy said. "You heard the slot of the dropoff box open, and then the video hit the inside of the collection cabinet. But the cabinet that the video falls onto is padded, so the noise sounds like a thud," she explained. "Kind of like a phantom would make." She raised her eyebrows.

"Cassy, we shouldn't joke about this. This is serious," the officer said as he tried to hide a smile.

Joe continued to read.

He had just reached the part where Leroux described the ghost. "'He is extraordinarily thin and his dress-coat hangs on a skeleton frame. His eyes are so deep that you can hardly see the fixed pupils. You just see two big black holes, as in a dead man's—'"

And then they heard a sound that wasn't a thud.

"Cassy, that wasn't a video," Officer Krulla whispered.

Joe hesitated, but then he peeked above the counter.

"It's nothing. It probably came from down the street," he said. "Someone can only enter through a door, and we'll be able to hear it open. And we have the element of surprise on our side. There's no reason to worry."

"Well, I'm still a little spooked," Cassy said. "I'm so glad you're here." She looked at Joe when she said this, as though Officer Krulla wasn't there at all. And Joe wished so much that Officer Krulla wasn't in the store.

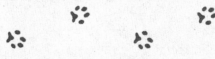

"Huh? Huh?" Wishbone said sleepily, whipping his head around to look around the store. The last sound had awakened him. "Did I miss anything?"

Noticing that everyone looked calm, Wishbone yawned and stretched out.

"I can hear someone approaching!" He raced around to the entrance door. "C'mon, be Ed!" Wishbone said excitedly.

But it wasn't Ed—it was Michael Menton, an actor who'd journeyed to worlds far away in science fiction films. *Or at least I think it is,* Wishbone thought. *Hey, down here! I'm perfect for an alien encounter of any kind!* The actor opened the video-return slot. Wishbone was so close, but yet so far away. A pane of glass was all that separated him from his extra-terrestrial dreams. He couldn't help but bark.

At first, the man looked startled when he noticed the dog. Then he smiled and waved, then turned and walked away.

"Wishbone! You're blowing our cover!" Joe said.

"But, Joe, you don't understand!" Wishbone pleaded. "I coulda—I coulda." He plopped down in disappointment. "I just know he's a Hollywood type."

"It's just Mr. Jolin," Officer Krulla said, as he saw the man walk away.

Mr. Jolin? Wishbone thought. *That's why he looked familiar—he's the science teacher who has an amazing resemblance to the actor.*

"Okay, Joe, back to the book," Cassy said excitedly.

Officer Krulla got up and stretched. "Hey, Cassy, I need to check in with the station. Can I use a phone?" he asked.

She stood up. "Sure," she said. "You can use the phone in the back office so you don't have to worry about our vandal hearing you. I'll unlock the office for you." She and the policeman got up, hunched over to hide themselves, and walked to the back of the store.

"Ahhhh!" The scream came from the back of the video store.

"Cassy, Cassy, are you all right?" Wishbone said, as he ran toward her, with Joe close behind.

They found Officer Krulla bent over, trying to calm himself down. Cassy was trying not to laugh.

"No problem, no problem," the policeman whispered. "I just saw this." He pointed to a life-sized cardboard display that stood in the back corner. "It startled me. But I'm okay now. Sorry to alarm everyone."

"No offense, Officer Krulla," Wishbone said. "But stakeouts may not be your strong point."

Joe and Wishbone returned to the front of the store and waited for Cassy and the policeman. "Get ready, pal," Wishbone said. "Cassy'll be back any second now."

Joe checked out his reflection in the window.

"You're looking good," Wishbone said. "Don't worry— I'd tell you if you didn't."

"Hey, guys," Cassy whispered. "What are you doing?"

"Eeks! Cassy, you scared me! Don't sneak up next time," Wishbone said, as he turned around.

"Oh, just . . . uh . . . looking outside, you know," Joe said unconvincingly.

Not such a good excuse, buddy, Wishbone thought.

"Well, let's get back to the book," Cassy said, as she sat down again. "I can't wait to find out what happens next."

Cassy snuggled up in a blanket she'd brought. "Come here, Wishbone," she said. "You look like you need your ears scratched."

"How well you know me," the dog said, as he trotted over to her.

"Uh . . . Cassy," Joe said.

"Yes?" she asked.

Here it comes, Wishbone thought. *Let's hope it goes according to plan.*

"I was thinking that maybe . . . you know . . . we could, sometime—" he began.

"Sorry, guys," Officer Krulla interrupted him. "But I'm needed back at the station."

Joe frowned.

"I know, I know, you were about to pop the question," Wishbone said. "But think about it this way—now you'll have even more time to ask her out!"

The policeman noticed Joe's disappointed look, too. "Now, son, don't you worry. I'll be back soon. And I'm sure you and Cassy can handle everything A-okay," he said, as he picked up his bag.

"You'll be back in a few minutes, right?" Cassy asked. "I mean, we'll be fine, but, you know—"

Officer Krulla patted her shoulder. "I will be back in less than fifteen minutes," he said, and he walked out the exit door.

Cassy stood up and locked it behind him. She watched as he walked around the corner and then drove by the front of the store shortly after. "I hope he hurries back," she said.

"We've got the stakeout all under control," Wishbone said. "No need for alarm." The dog could tell Cassy was uneasy. After sitting down again, she scratched his ears with a nervous energy.

"Okay, Joe," Wishbone said. "Begin plan 'Ask Cassy Out.'"

"*Aaaaah!*" A scream came from somewhere outside.

"What was that? That's not in the plan!" Wishbone said, startled.

Another yell came from deep in the night's darkness.

"Joe!" Cassy said. "What was that?"

He gulped. "I don't know," he said. "It sounded like a scream."

"I know that! But where do you think it came from? And who was it? And why?" Cassy asked. "I sure wish Officer Krulla hadn't left!"

"Just when I was getting cozy," Wishbone said. "Oh, well. This is what I was trained to do. Let's go, Joe."

Joe dropped his book and stood up. "I'm going outside to investigate," he said.

"Don't, Joe!" Cassy said. "You might end up in a dangerous situation."

"I've got to go check it out," Joe said, as he grabbed the policeman's flashlight.

"Let's wait for Officer Krulla to get back," Cassy said.

"Somebody might be in a lot of trouble and need our help now," Joe said. "We don't have time to wait."

"You're right," she said.

"Joe, you take the lead," Wishbone said. "I'll stay behind you and keep watch in the rear."

Unlocking the door, Joe headed out into the darkness. He shivered as Cassy wrapped her blanket tightly around her shoulders.

"Brrr!" Wishbone said. "It's chilly and spooky. Not my two favorite things."

The dog looked up at the dark sky. Clouds hid the stars and the moon. A single, lonely beam from the small flashlight Joe held was the only light other than a faint glow coming from the streetlights. The street they'd walked up and down so many times took on a different cast. What normally looked like an ordinary fire hydrant seemed scary in the black of night.

Wishbone thought he saw someone—or something—scuttle across the street in front of them. "A giant insect? Joe, did you see that?" he said.

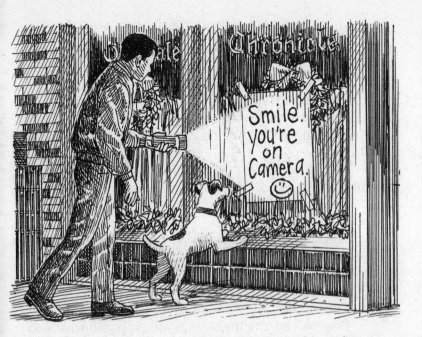

"Help!" Another shriek pierced the cold night air. Cassy grabbed Joe's arm and screamed.

Joe put his arm around Cassy's shoulder and squeezed it to reassure her.

"Don't forget about me!" Wishbone said. "I'm frightened, too!"

They started running toward the yelling sounds. It seemed as if the noise was coming from the building that housed *The Oakdale Chronicle*.

Joe got a few steps ahead of Cassy and the dog and stopped in front of the newspaper office's door.

"What is it what is it what is it?" Wishbone asked, making his way around Joe to peek.

A piece of posterboard was propped up against the window. On it was written in blood-red letters:

Smile. You're on camera.

A smiley face was drawn underneath the words.

"My heart is beating a million times a second," Cassy said. "This is a prank? I thought someone was hurt."

"Hey, guys," Wishbone said, "we're being watched."

Joe turned and looked down the dark street. He couldn't make anything out. "Where do you think the prankster could be?" he said.

"Who knows? Let's get back to the store," Cassy said. "This could be a trick to get us away from the place."

"You're right!" Wishbone ran back to The Movie Shoppe.

Officer Krulla drove up just as they reached the store. He hurried out of his car. "What happened? Where'd you go?" he asked.

"You'll never believe it," Wishbone said. "We had quite a little adventure."

They walked into the store as Joe explained what had happened.

"We're out of here, guys," Cassy said. "The vandal is just playing with us. Incredible."

"The vandal knows we're here," Officer Krulla said. "And the culprit is not going to do anything that will get him or her caught tonight."

Joe sighed.

"Officer Krulla is right, Joe," Wishbone said. "And after that scare, I wouldn't mind being tucked safe and sound in my bed."

He noticed Cassy was packing up the food.

"On second thought, maybe I could stay for a snack," he said. *Would it be impolite for me to ask for a doggie bag? Wishbone thought. Maybe I'll just see if Officer Krulla knows where an all-night doughnut store is. If anybody knows, it would be him.*

Chapter Eleven

Wednesday at eleven, Cassy, Joe, and Wishbone were back at work. Joe had his Santa hat on, and Wishbone had his holiday dog collar on. Cassy threw a newspaper down on the video store counter. "Just look at this," she said to Joe. "Your dog is a star!"

Wishbone's face gazed out from the front page of the college newspaper. The headline read:

DOG INVADES STUDENT UNION

Below that was a picture of Dr. Meacham, with a stain on his coat. The caption underneath it read:

REPORT HIM TO THE POUND—THAT'S WHAT I'LL DO!

"Hey, little buddy," Cassy said, scratching Wishbone behind the ears. "What kind of trouble did you get yourself into?" she asked.

"I wonder when he was at the union," Joe said. "This must have been when he disappeared for a while yesterday. I wonder what he was looking for."

Cassy smiled and walked to the back of the store.

Joe read the article. Fortunately, Wishbone had not broken anything. He had just startled a few people, especially Dr. Meacham. The security guard was quoted as saying that dogs were not allowed in the cafeteria, and he was just trying to remove Wishbone. A student was quoted as saying that she was glad the school had finally admitted a member of the highly intelligent canine species. Joe laughed. He looked at Wishbone and smiled.

Joe had been so certain the vandal would have been caught last night. *Ed is the culprit! I just know it. How am I ever going to prove it was Ed?* Joe wondered.

Joe's mom walked in. He had told her at breakfast what had happened last night. "Hi, Joe!" she said. "The hat sure looks festive!"

"Hi, Mom!" he said. Then he lowered his voice. "Just one more day and it's retired for a year. The store is not open Christmas Eve." He smiled. "Did you come to rent a movie?"

Cassy saw Joe's mom and headed toward her.

"Mrs. Talbot! Hi! You're early!" she said.

Joe was confused. "Early?" he asked. "Early for what?"

Cassy grabbed her backpack. "Your mom came by a few days ago and asked me to lunch. Today's the day," she said. "You'll be okay alone for a while, won't you?" she asked.

"Yeah, sure," Joe said.

"Order a pizza," Cassy suggested. "Maybe Sam will come by and deliver it."

Ellen smiled and followed Cassy out the door. "See you in about an hour!" she said.

If last night had gone as planned, I'd be the one eating with Cassy, Joe thought. Joe put one of his favorite holiday movies in the VCR. It made him feel less uncomfortable about the Santa hat on his head. He watched the movie as he reshelved some videos. His right wrist was feeling better. A few customers came in, and he helped them.

He decided to take Cassy's suggestion and he dialed Pepper Pete's. Sam picked up.

"Hey!" he said. "I'm at work. Come over with a pizza and we'll have lunch."

"First I've got to ask my dad," she said. "But I'm up for it."

Sam got her father's permission, and Joe called David, too.

They soon came, Sam with pizza and David with soft drinks.

"Are you sure Cassy won't mind?" Sam said.

"Not at all. In fact, she suggested it," Joe answered.

"Like I said before," David said, as he picked up a slice, "you have the best boss ever. How'd last night's stakeout go?"

"Not so well," Joe said. He told them about the stakeout. But he wasn't ready yet to tell his friends that he was going to ask Cassy out. He thought he'd wait until after she said yes.

They ate and watched a movie. No customers came in for a while.

Then Damont arrived. "Working hard, I see," he said. "And you get paid for this?"

"Hi, Damont," Joe said. "You want to rent a movie?"

"What I want to do," Damont answered, "is eat pizza, watch videos, and get paid to do it. Joe, do you have any ideas about how I could do that?" He picked up a video and pretended to read the label.

"Damont, what are you doing over the holiday break?" Sam asked.

Damont faked a shot. "Basketball practice is using up most of my days," he said. "I don't have a lot of time for, you know, sitting around with my friends. By the way, Joe," he said, "how's that wrist?"

"Better, Damont. Thanks for asking," Joe replied. He touched the bandage on his wrist.

"Well, while I hate to leave your little party, I've got plans," Damont said. Just as he was about to walk out the door, he tossed the movie he had been looking at on the counter. "There, Joe," he said. "Put that up. It'll give you something to do." He then walked through the exit door.

They waited until he was out of sight before speaking.

"He's in his usual good humor today," David commented.

"I wonder what's bugging him," Sam said. She always tried to find an excuse for Damont's behavior.

Joe tapped his fingers on the counter. "He might be trying to get back at me. Remember last Saturday, when Cassy turned him down for a job? He looked upset."

"That was four days ago! Would he be holding a grudge that long?" Sam asked.

"When you hurt Damont's ego," David said, "you never know what you're in for." He paused for a minute. "Maybe *he's* the guy, Joe. Maybe he's the one who's been taping people."

Joe thought about it for a second. "Damont could be responsible, but I still think it's Ed," he said.

"So have you gotten any more proof?" Sam asked.

"No," Joe said. He explained what had happened yesterday when Officer Krulla had spoken to Dr. Meacham. "The security tape proves that he's innocent. But I just know he's not. It's like in *The Phantom of the Opera*."

Although Sam had already read the book and David was reading it, they didn't seem to make the connection.

"You know, the Phantom gets mad because the new managers won't satisfy his requests," Joe began.

"Yes, that's right. And then he starts to sabotage the theater," Sam continued.

They looked at David to see if he was following along. He was eating a slice of pizza. "I wouldn't know," he said. "I haven't gotten to that part yet."

Sam smiled. "At first it's just little stuff. Noises, laughter during performances, demands for a box seat. But the theater managers continue to refuse his requests. And then—this really gets the Phantom angry—they replace his beloved Christine with her rival, even though he warns them not to. So it gets worse—"

Joe interrupted her. "—when Christine disappears, Raoul, the man who loves her, has no idea where's she's gone."

"I was actually going to say that the Phantom kills a woman in the audience by dropping a chandelier on her," Sam said. "But Christine does disappear, too."

"And that's why I think it's Ed. He's got the motive, revenge, and the means, access to high-tech equipment," Joe said. "I've just got to prove it, like the narrator in the book proves the Phantom really exists."

"You'd better prove he's the vandal before he does anything worse," David said.

"I'm not expecting a falling chandelier," Joe said. "But after last night, who knows what might happen next?" Joe said. "Sam, I just noticed there's a message on the answering machine. You're closest to the machine. Could you push Play? Cassy must have forgotten to check the messages this morning."

She did. After a bit of whirring, the messages started to play.

"You have one new message: ten-forty-five A.M. today— Hey, honey! It's Mom. I'm calling to check up on last night's stakeout. I hope you had fun playing detective! Be sure and call me later on. Call me on my cell phone. Gotta go, sweetie— the cameras are about to start rolling! Talk to you later."

"That was right before we opened at eleven," Joe said.

"We know a *little* more about Cassy's mom now," David said. "She's got a cell phone, and she's got to run when the cameras are rolling. Maybe she's a famous actress!"

"It would be so cool if her mom was a Hollywood star," Sam said. "I'll save the message so Cassy can hear it when she gets back."

"Miss Bennett didn't sound too concerned," Joe said. "That's kind of strange, because Cassy said she might close the store because of all the problems."

David almost choked on his pizza. "What?" he said. "You didn't tell us that! Why?"

"It's this vandalism," Joe replied. "Cassy says her mom is already very stressed, and she won't want to have to deal with this, too."

"But she sounded so cheerful," Sam said. "Miss Bennett said she hoped Cassy had fun."

"I know," Joe said. "A contradiction."

"Joe, no one's ever seen Miss Bennett, right?" David asked.

"Not anyone I know, except for Cassy," Joe said. "Why?"

"What do we know about Miss Bennett?" David asked. "Cassy says her mom is stressed out and nervous about the vandalism in the store. Based on the message her mom left on the answering machine, she's happy and was not very concerned about the stakeout last night. Is this the same person?"

"What's your point, David?" Joe asked.

"Someone is not telling the truth," David said.

Joe knew David was right. But he refused even to think about what David was saying.

"Maybe one of the Bennetts is behind this," David said.

"Why would either one vandalize the video store?" Sam asked.

"Maybe Cassy's mom really doesn't want the store to succeed. Or maybe Cassy is angry at her mom for being away and is getting back at her," David proposed. "I don't know."

"It's a bad theory," Wishbone said. "No offense, David. Cassy's mom? No one who could make such a delicious cookie would be capable of doing such evil deeds. Cassy? She appreciates the finer things in life. Speaking of finer things, let's give the dog some more pizza down here." Wishbone gave Sam a hungry look.

"Joe, you do have to admit Cassy's behavior has been a little weird," David said.

"Okay, I'll give you that," Wishbone said, "*if* you give me another piece of the pizza."

Sam looked down at Wishbone and gave him a piece of pizza crust.

"Thank you," Wishbone said as he chewed. He then yawned and stretched.

Joe hadn't responded to David's remarks. The three kids just stood around silently.

"Well, I've got to get back to work," Sam said, as she put the empty pizza box in the trash can under the counter.

"I should be going, too," David said, looking uncomfortable. "I'll walk you back to the restaurant, Sam."

"Thanks for the pizza," Joe said. He didn't look at David.

"Yes, thanks for the pizza!" Wishbone said. "It was one of your dad's best ever, Sam."

A few minutes after Sam and David left the store, Cassy returned.

112

"Hey, guys!" Cassy said, walking in. "How's it going? Have you had lunch?"

"Great to see you!" Wishbone greeted her. "I'm absolutely starved. It's been almost ten minutes since I've eaten. You didn't happen to bring a doggie bag, did you?"

"It's going well, Cassy. A few customers. But no problems, and Sam and David just brought over a pizza," Joe answered.

"Great, Joe," Cassy said. "Lunch was so much fun. Your mom is really nice."

"Yes," he said. "She is."

"Ellen! She's great and . . ." Wishbone stopped. Joe was looking at Cassy with a puzzled expression. *He's thinking about what David had said.*

Joe, the Bennetts are innocent. Call it gut instinct, Wishbone thought.

"We had a really good time," Cassy continued. "I'm glad I finally met her."

"I hope I can meet your mom soon, too," Joe said. Pointing at the answering machine, he said, "There's a message from her on the machine."

"Oh, really?" Cassy said, as she walked over to it. "What did she have to say?"

"Oh, nothing . . . just . . . I saved it," Joe stammered.

Cassy played the message.

"Well, that's my mom!" she said. "One positive woman. But she works too hard."

"By the way, what does she do?" Joe asked. "I don't think you've ever told me."

"You'll find out one of these days," Cassy teased good-naturedly.

"I'm guessing she's a professional chef," Wishbone said. "Just a thought."

"Let's play another movie. How about this one?" Cassy

handed Joe a movie that had just been returned. "It's one of my favorites."

"Now, if you'd just pop us some popcorn, we'd be set," Wishbone said.

Joe put the tape into the master VCR and pushed Play. As the trailers rolled by, he took a deep breath.

"Now's the perfect time, buddy! She's in a great mood, and she's met your mom," Wishbone said. "Ask away!"

"Cassy . . ." Joe said, his voice squeaking nervously. He coughed.

"Yes, Joe? What's up?" she asked with a smile.

"I was thinking that maybe . . . you know . . . if you wanted to, we could—" he began.

"Joe, look at that," Cassy said, interrupting him, pointing to the viewing monitor.

David and Sam walked in at the same time. "Hey!" David said. "We're back! I forgot my hat." He looked up at the screen, which Cassy was pointing to.

A sign for The Movie Shoppe appeared on the screen in place of the movie.

"Hey! Look! It's us," Wishbone said.

It was a scene from only about an hour ago. Sam and David had just arrived with the pizza. Joe and his friends were laughing and eating pizza.

Then the screen went dark, except for a single beam of light that kept moving back and forth. It took Wishbone a few moments to realize what was on the screen.

"We *were* on camera last night!" he said. "There *was* someone out there in the dark!"

Cassy took the tape out of the VCR. "No!" she said. "This can't have happened again! It just *can't.*"

Joe took the tape from her hand. "He's working fast—real fast," he said. "That pizza scene was only an hour ago."

"I saw Dr. Meacham and Mr. Miller in front of the store

just before I went to lunch," Cassy said, sounding panicky. "And Damont Jones just a minute or two later. It must be one of them who altered the film."

Sam went over to Cassy and put an arm around her shoulders. "We'll figure this out. It's going to be okay."

"How could someone have done this without us noticing?" Joe said. "At the same time that we were talking about him, he was taping us."

"And someone was *watching* us last night," Cassy said. "It wasn't just a prank."

Wishbone saw the fear on Cassy's face. Joe must have noticed it, too.

Joe said, "Cassy, I'm going to catch this guy. I'm going to bust this guy and save this store."

Joe looked at his watch. "It's three o'clock," he said. "I'm sure they're still at school," Joe said, almost to himself. "I'll be back in an hour or so, Cassy."

Then Joe looked at Sam and David.

He said to his best friends, "I'm going over to Oakdale College. Want to come along?"

They both said yes.

"Come on, Wishbone," Joe said, as Sam and David followed him out the exit door.

"Watch out, whoever you are! Here we come!" Wishbone said.

Chapter Twelve

Joe knocked on the professor's office door. He heard movement inside. "Dr. Meacham, this is Joe Talbot. I have to talk to you." Joe was too determined to solve this case to be nervous about how the professor would react to his unexpected visit.

David and Sam, however, were a bit more hesitant. They stood quietly behind their friend.

The professor opened the door. "I'm quite busy," he said, pushing his glasses down on his nose and looking at Wishbone and then Joe. "But I suppose I can talk for a moment." He seemed to sense that Joe would not take no for an answer. "Come in."

The professor sat in a chair behind his desk. "So what can I do for you, Joe?" The man pointed to a group of chairs. "Sit down, all of you."

Joe told him that the tape vandalism had continued. And he explained that it now threatened the store itself. Joe hesitated before making his next point. "I think I know who's behind it, but I can't prove it without your help."

Professor Meacham looked at Joe for a few seconds. "I admire your determination. This vandal must be stopped.

Who knows who the next victim could be?" And although his words were serious, his voice quaked. He was nervous, and Joe wasn't sure why.

"I need you to tell me if Ed Baines has used the editing equipment within the last two hours. The latest tape we received had footage that was shot over two hours ago," Joe said.

Dr. Meacham fumbled with papers on his desk for a minute before speaking. "I do have information that may help you," the professor said.

A long pause followed.

Joe had a crazy thought—*What if it* was *Dr. Meacham?* He was acting strangely, as though he had something to confess.

Joe spoke up. "Professor Meacham, what is it?"

"I should have told Officer Krulla when he was here yesterday," the man said. "I refused to believe there was a connection. I refused to admit one of my students could be involved."

Is he talking about Ed? Joe thought.

The professor stood up and began to pace. "This could still be a coincidence," he said. "I had no bad intentions in this matter," the professor said, as he sat down in his chair again.

"Of course you didn't," Joe said. He didn't know if he believed that, but he wanted Dr. Meacham to hurry up and talk.

The professor put both his hands on the desk and looked at Joe earnestly. Joe leaned toward him. Sam and David held their breath.

"Ed Baines has checked out a video camera recently. Several times, in fact," the professor admitted.

Sam sighed with relief. David almost fell over.

"I knew it was him!" Joe said.

"Whew! Joe was right all along. That's my boy!" Wishbone said. "Glad to hear you're not the guy, Dr. Meacham. You're starting to grow on me."

The professor looked relieved after his confession. "But the security camera in the film library shows he's been in there almost constantly for the past few days," the professor admitted. "Although he's been acting quite strangely, I don't see how he could have been at the library and videotaping his victims at the same time."

"That is exactly what we're here to figure out," Wishbone said.

"Where do you think Ed is now?" Joe asked.

"The film library—of course," the professor said. "If you'll turn to my television, I can access the security camera in the library."

Joe walked behind the desk to get a better view of the screen.

The professor pushed a few buttons, and an image of the film library popped up on the screen. "There he is now," he said. "Filing away. It's amazing there's enough work to keep him that busy."

How does he do it? Joe thought. *Somehow he's managing to be at several places at the same time.*

Joe leaned against the window frame in Dr. Meacham's office and stared at the tape. Ed worked carefully as he placed books and videos on shelves.

"Illusion," Joe said after a few seconds.

"What are you thinking?" Sam said.

"You remember what happens in *The Phantom of the Opera?* The Phantom created an illusion room full of mirrors,"

Joe said. "And then he locks up his victims in it to drive them crazy."

"Just like Ed's doing to us," David said.

"Well, there's one way to find out if it's an illusion or not," Joe said. He turned to Professor Meacham. "Where's the library? Can we go there?"

"Of course," Professor Meacham said. "Just follow me."

He stood up and walked out of his office. The group made its way down the hall to the library. A student sat at a desk just outside the room, reading a textbook. Professor Meacham walked up to him.

"Here we are," the professor said. "Good afternoon, Frank. We're here to see Ed."

"No one's in the library, Dr. Meacham," the student replied. "And Ed hasn't been here for days. I've heard that he's practically been living in editing room number two."

"But that can't be," the professor said. "I just saw him on the film library security tape!"

"I've worked here all week, and I haven't seen him," Frank said, setting his book down.

Joe opened the door to the library and walked in. Sam and David followed him. Just as Frank had said, it was empty. Suddenly, Joe knew he had been right all along. Ed was the one they were looking for. He was altering the tapes, and he had somehow figured out a way around the security camera. He used the camera to avoid being caught. Joe had a pretty good idea of how he had done that, too.

He looked around the room, searching for the camera. He could hear the professor arguing with Frank. Then he and Frank walked inside the library.

"He's not in here!" the professor said after he looked around the room. "This security system is useless."

"Professor, you had Ed install the system," Frank said quietly.

Dr. Meacham looked at him and frowned. "I know how he did it. With all my film experience, I'm surprised I didn't realize this sooner. I'd get up to where the camera is mounted and look at it, but— Joe, can you do it?" he asked.

Joe pulled a chair up to the camera. He climbed up on the chair. "It's all hooked up and—" he said as he fiddled with the camera. He followed the connection back to the wall and carefully removed the panel where the wires were. There it was—a VCR with the Play button blinking.

Here is the key to the illusion, Joe told himself. *The Phantom's revealed himself.*

He unplugged the machine and brought it down to Dr. Meacham. He ejected the tape. "If we play this, I'm pretty sure it will be a looped tape of what you've been seeing on the security camera."

"I know where there's a VCR nearby," Dr. Meacham said. "Editing room number two. The room Ed usually uses."

They thanked Frank and followed Dr. Meacham back down the hall. "How can this be?" he muttered to himself. He knocked on a door. "Ed, it's Dr. Meacham," he said. He opened the door before Ed had a chance to respond.

Or to change the tape he was working on. Dr. Meacham was greeted by his face on the screen. "What's this?" he asked incredulously.

Joe made his way into the room. He remained silent.

"Ed, what is this?" Dr. Meacham asked. "I demand an answer!"

The suspect sat frozen in the chair. He was speechless.

"Well, then, let's see what's on this tape," Dr. Meacham said. The tape was in Pause mode. He pushed Play.

The screen showed Dr. Meacham sitting in his office, in front of his television. He looked to be enjoying himself immensely. And then the camera panned to the TV screen he was watching.

It was an unexpected sight: Dr. Meacham was not watching a documentary, a historical drama, or even a made-for-TV movie. It was a game show.

The tape panned back to Dr. Meacham. He looked as though he was having the time of his life. Joe had not seen this side of the professor.

"Yes, even *I* need to relax my mind every so often," the professor defended himself. "There is no crime in watching, shall we say, 'silly' television once in a while. I admit," he said, looking at David, "that I might have been overly critical of David when he was exercising while at his job, but now I understand—"

"Because it was *you* who was caught!" Ed snarled. All eyes turned to this angry figure. "That's what happened to me! Cassy found me leaving the store, just once, and she fired me. This could happen to anyone! We all slack off once in a while. Officer Krulla eats doughnuts, David jumps around doing exercises, Joe parties with his friends, and even Dr. Meacham watches a game show! All during work hours! But I'm the only one gets fired!" Ed protested.

Dr. Meacham cleared his throat. "While you seem to be quite fond of your rationalization," he said, "it has some faults."

Joe was glad the confident, arrogant Dr. Meacham had returned—as long as his wrath wasn't direct at Joe and his friends.

"Let me explain my actions first," he continued. "It is perfectly acceptable, if not a bit embarrassing, that I watch a frivolous television show if I choose. I have certain liberties as a professor, and this is one I choose to take. And I've discovered that David, as well, was taking a well-deserved break."

"And Officer Krulla," Sam piped in. "He'd just gotten off a ten-hour shift."

Ed didn't look convinced.

122

"I did have friends over to eat lunch and watch a movie," Joe said. "But Cassy was okay with that, and I never left the store."

"Slacking off is slacking off. I don't care about your excuses," Ed said.

"You will care once you confess everything to the police," Joe said.

"Ugh!" Ed said.

"I assume we already know what's on this tape," Dr. Meacham said. He held the tape from the library security camera in his hand.

"Yeah, yeah," Ed said. "The looped tape of myself working in the library. I didn't figure you'd ever notice that I was filing the same video over and over."

"Pretty sneaky, getting the time code to work and all," David said.

"I was taught by the best," Ed answered, motioning to Dr. Meacham.

"But I never taught you to be deceitful, however," the professor said.

Joe didn't feel like he'd gotten to the very bottom of things yet. There were still a few loose ends. He remembered his phone call to the Baines house, and Mark's appearance at the video store. "Hey, Ed," he said. "Where's your little brother, by the way?"

Ed didn't answer.

Joe looked around the room and noticed a shadow in the corner. Taking a few steps, he saw Mark. The boy came out of the corner once he realized Joe had discovered him.

"You *are* just like the Phantom!" Sam said.

"What does that mean?" Ed asked.

"It's a character in a book," Sam replied.

"And what exactly is your role in this tomfoolery?" Dr. Meacham said, looking at Mark.

"Tomfoolery?" Ed said sarcastically. "That word went extinct about a million years ago."

"I think it best you take this a little more seriously, young man," the professor said to Ed.

"Have you been in on this since the beginning?" Joe asked Mark. "Or just since my phone call?"

"The phone call. I told Ed I'd tell Mom unless he let me help," Mark said.

"So that's how Ed managed to seem like he's at several places at the same time," Joe said.

"That was pretty risky—vandalizing a tape you'd checked out and claiming it wasn't your fault," Joe said.

"But how did you get *my* tape?" the professor asked.

"I sneaked it out of your office," Ed said quietly.

"Excuse me?" the professor roared. "You broke into my office and took my property!"

"He didn't break in—it was unlocked while you were in class. And he returned the tape later," Mark said.

"After conveniently vandalizing it. Ed, you'll be back in my office after you have spoken with the police. Cassy also deserves to be told in person. And then you will be in the dean's office," Dr. Meacham said. Mark giggled. Dr. Meacham turned to him. "As will you, my young friend."

"Mark, just be quite now. No more confessions, okay? Let me do the talking," Ed said.

"You'll be doing some talking, and confessing, at the video store. Now let's go," Joe said.

Ed hesitated and then grabbed his jacket. "Let's get this over with."

They stood up and left the small editing room. Ed and his brother, Mark, led the group, and Joe left the room last. Dr. Meacham slowed his pace so he could walk beside Joe.

"What a dramatic afternoon," Dr. Meacham said.

Joe nodded his head.

"So, Joe, I'm intrigued by Sam's comment about Mark being the Phantom," the professor said. "I assume that's a reference to the French classic by Gaston Leroux."

"Yes, it is," Joe said. "We're reading it for English class. It's a pretty great book."

"I've enjoyed the film versions many times," the professor said. "And I agree with you—it does seem to resemble this situation in many ways."

Joe nodded in agreement.

"Let's see if I have this correct. Ed represents the Phantom. I assume Cassy is Christine. And Raoul? Would that be you, Joe?" the professor said with a smile.

Joe's face turned red, and he stared at his shoes. He stammered over a couple of words, but nothing intelligible came out.

Professor Meacham stopped in front of his office door. "I won't be accompanying you to the video store. I'll call Officer Krulla and tell him to meet you at the store. I'll also call Cassy to let her know you'll be arriving," he said. "I've got some work to attend to. I'm glad I could be of help."

Joe caught up with David.

"Let's make sure Ed and Mark don't try to slip away before confessing," Joe said, as the group left the building.

Chapter Thirteen

Wishbone was proud of Joe. He had solved the case almost singlehandedly. The terrier was walking down the stairs in front of the film building with his friends when he saw *the* woman.

He'd experienced a few cases of mistaken identity in the last few days. But when he saw *the* woman head toward the auditorium, he knew she was for real.

"It's Ginger Johnson—the award-winning-theater-star-turned-Oscar-winning-film-actress! And she's entering the auditorium—it all makes perfect sense," Wishbone said. "Sorry, guys, but this might be my only chance! I'll be back in just a minute!" he said to his friends as he darted off. He knew he could catch up with the group afterward.

The auditorium. A good place to see and be seen, Wishbone thought.

Wishbone had become a master of disguises over the years. One of his famous roles was as Stealth Dog. Stealth Dog could dissolve into the scenery, become invisible, disappear into the woodwork. *The time at the student union was just a fluke,* he thought. And so he blended in.

But then he heard someone ask, "Hey, isn't that the

dog that was in the paper a few days ago? He's the one who caused all the excitement in the student union."

He darted into the building before hearing the answer. *I'll sign autographs later,* he told himself. *But for now, I've got to track Miss Johnson.*

I've always known I had a flair for drama, Wishbone thought. *I should have known that this was the perfect category of acting for me.*

Making his way through the auditorium lobby, he tried to avoid getting noticed. But he got noticed, nonetheless. He soon realized that, on the Oakdale College campus, at least, he was a star.

"Look—he's the one who got Dr. Meacham so upset the other day," a student said.

Another student reached down and patted him. "Hey, pup! I saw you in the paper! Way to go!" he said.

"Yeah," someone else said. "I've never seen Dr. Meacham lose his cool."

But Wishbone could spare no time for admiration. He followed the starlet into the house—the seating part of the auditorium.

The lights were dim in the house, except on the stage. The stage was brightly lit, and a class sat on the floor, awaiting their teacher. And it seems that Ginger Johnson could do a very good impersonation of a Professor Winsey. At least, all the students greeted her by that name when she walked in.

Wishbone watched *the* woman for a few minutes. He had to be honest with himself. "Okay, so she's not a world-famous actress," Wishbone said, as he sat on a seat in the auditorium's front row. "But she probably is an actress, and maybe I can learn something while I'm here."

"Close your eyes, and imagine an orange in your hand," the teacher was saying. "Round. Solid. Bumpy. A navel on top. Can you feel it?"

Some of the students closed their eyes tightly. A few raised their hands, with their fingers curled, as if around an actual orange. And others, like Wishbone, just weren't getting it.

"An orange? Can't we imagine something else? A pizza—now, that's a food I can imagine," Wishbone said.

One of the equally unconvinced students was squinting and looking in the direction of the front row of seats. He noticed the dog. "That's the dog from the school paper!" he said.

"We're supposed to be thinking about *oranges* here, not dogs," the teacher said.

"But there's a star in our midst, Professor Winsey. He made headlines!" the student said, as he stood up. "Come up here, little buddy!" he said.

Wishbone stayed where he was. He wanted to be sure he wouldn't be replaying the scene from the cafeteria.

The professor stood up. "Come here, little doggie!" she said.

He considered her words a hall pass. "Well, if you *insist,* but I wish you'd drop 'little,'" he said.

The class livened up immediately as Wishbone made his way onstage. He heard whispers all around him.

"He's a natural," Professor Winsey said. "Who is he?"

"Over here, little guy," a girl in the corner said. "You're cute as can be."

"Cute? He's *fabulous!*" the professor said. "Class, I think we've found what we're looking for—a replacement for Dingo."

"You have!" Wishbone said. "I'm a star waiting to happen!" Wishbone looked back at the professor. "So who's Dingo?"

"Professor Winsey, he'd be wonderful," a student mentioned.

"You're right!" another student answered.

Finally, the recognition and admiration I've been waiting for! Wishbone thought.

Joe didn't want to leave campus without his dog. Wishbone might end up on the front page of *The Oakdale Chronicle* next time.

He looked at his watch. It was five o'clock—later than he thought. Joe had seen Wishbone leave the group and head toward the auditorium. The boy told the group to wait for him while he went to get Wishbone. He'd be right back.

He entered the auditorium. Joe asked a student whether she had seen a dog, and she pointed to two double doors. Joe entered and proceeded to the stage slowly, curious as to what was going on.

Wishbone commanded center stage, as usual.

"Hey Joe!" he said. "They love me! They really love me!"

"Are you here to claim this animal?" the professor asked. "Because I'm not letting him leave until you promise me you'll bring him back. We've got a walk-on role for a dog in our new play. But our little Labrador, Dingo, got sick. We're hoping this delightful canine can replace him. Opening night is in two weeks."

"Joe! I'm going to be a star!" Wishbone said.

Joe laughed. "Yes, he's my dog, and, yes, he can take part in your play," he said. "Wishbone would enjoy that."

"Tomorrow morning at nine o'clock sharp we start rehearsals. I expect to see him there!" the professor said.

"Who'd have thought?" Wishbone said. "Now, back to you, Joe. We've just got to get you a date with Cassy!"

Chapter Fourteen

"I found him!" Joe announced to the group. They'd been waiting on the outside steps of the film building for Joe to return, hopefully with Wishbone. "You won't believe where he was," he continued.

"Let me guess," David said as he bent down and scratched the dog's head. "Up onstage, commanding all the attention with a Shakespearean monologue."

David's answer surprised Joe. "Yes, you're right," Joe said. "Well, not about Shakespeare, but he was onstage. Wishbone landed himself a role in a play."

"Someone must have an eye for talent," Sam said.

David gave Joe a thumbs-up.

Wishbone was so busy enjoying all the attention that he didn't notice the girl walking by.

"See her?" Sam whispered to Joe, elbowing his side. "I think that's Hilary Morgan Cooper. Rumor has it she's attending school here, but she doesn't want anyone to know. She's trying to avoid publicity."

"Wow!" Joe said. "That'd be pretty cool if that is her."

"Even if it isn't her, it looks a whole lot like her," David said.

"It sure does," Joe said.

"See how you can easily get confused? I've been seeing people who look like famous actors, too," Wishbone said.

The group was almost at the video store. "Ed and Mark, so how'd you do it?" Wishbone said. "Because while I don't admire your actions, I do admire your technique."

They were not paying attention to Wishbone. Instead, Mark tried to talk to his brother. "You know, I didn't screw anything up, Ed," he was saying. "It was all that time in the editing room. I *told* you we should have found another place."

"Mark, I really don't need this right now," Ed said.

"But what are Mom and Dad going to say? I think we're going to be in a lot of trouble," Mark continued. "What are we going to do?"

Ed just ignored him.

"Mark, Ed, down here! I'm talking to you," Wishbone said.

"At least we'll go through it together, right?" Mark pleaded. Ed still said nothing. "We're a team, right?"

Mark finally noticed Wishbone. "Hey, guy!" he said. "I remember you—you were with the stakeout group last night!"

"That was me!" Wishbone and the group arrived at the video store and entered. "Here we are," Wishbone said.

Cassy's eyes opened up wide when she saw the group enter. "Dr. Meacham called and explained what happened." She looked at Ed. "So it was you! Joe was right all along!" she said. She walked out from behind the counter and approached Joe.

"Way to go!" She gave him a hug.

Ed stood at the back of the group, his head down.

"And as for you," she said, pointing to Ed, "you're in lots of trouble. I can't even begin to express just how much trouble you're in."

"I know, I know," Ed said. "I'm in lots of trouble, yadda-yadda-yadda. I've heard this all before."

"Oh, no," she said. "You *think* you've heard all this before. But you haven't. What's coming is much worse."

"Ooh, I'm scared," he said.

A siren went off, and the reflection of flashing police lights filled the store.

Ed turned around nervously. "What's this?" he asked.

"Weren't you listening to Cassy? It's the 'much worse punishment,'" Wishbone said.

"It's the police, Ed," Cassy said.

Officer Krulla walked in the door. "Well, Ed," he said. "So it was you, after all?"

"Boy, you're in trouble," Mark said. "The police, Ed. That's *serious*. And wait till Mom and Dad hear."

"Hello, young man," Officer Krulla said to Mark. "Good to see you again. Fill me in, Joe," he said.

"And don't forget my starring role, either," Wishbone said.

"I've always thought Ed was behind this," Joe began, "even though the evidence showed otherwise. After viewing the third vandalized tape and seeing how upset and scared Cassy was, I decided I had to talk to Dr. Meacham again. He was holding back information that I felt could help us. The next person I needed to talk to was Ed, on his own turf—at the film school. I couldn't let the video store close, or have Cassy go through this anymore," he said.

Cassy blushed.

"Trust me, Cassy," Wishbone said. "He wasn't going to let it happen again."

"And when Professor Meacham let me into the library, I found Ed had rigged up the camera to make it look like he was in there the entire time. Which allowed him time to videotape his victims. We even caught him red-handed with a secretly filmed video of Dr. Meacham," Joe said.

"I'm so impressed," Cassy said, looking at Joe. "I never would have made it through this week without you."

Wishbone noticed the admiring look in Cassy's eyes. "Don't forget, you're going to ask her out, buddy!" he said to Joe.

Just as Cassy was about to hug Joe, the front door opened and a boy about twenty years old walked in.

"Could you wait just a second?" Wishbone said. "You're kind of interrupting a special moment."

Cassy turned from Joe and ran to the guy. She put her

arms around his neck and gave him a kiss. "Bill!" she gushed. "I'm so glad you're finally here!"

"Stay cool, stay cool," Wishbone said to Joe. "Maybe there's a good explanation."

"Joe, meet Bill, my boyfriend," Cassy introduced the two.

"Nope," Wishbone said. "Not a good explanation at all."

Chapter Fifteen

"**B**ill! Cassy!" Joe called to the couple. "We're over here!" They were outside the college auditorium building to see Wishbone's stage debut.

Ellen grabbed her coat from the Ford Explorer's front seat. "Is that Cassy's boyfriend, Joe?" she asked.

"Yes, that's Bill," Joe said, as he shut the Explorer's door. "Cassy met him at Oakdale College. They've been dating for a couple of months."

The day Ed and Mark were taken to the police station by Officer Krulla, Joe and Wishbone finally arrived home exhausted. Joe ate a quick dinner and told his mom about his day. He mentioned Bill. She didn't ask any questions other than to inquire if Joe was all right. A few days later he talked to David and Sam about Cassy.

Joe and his mom met up with Cassy and Bill and headed toward the building. After introducing Bill to Mrs. Talbot, Cassy made her way back over to Joe. They walked together to the entrance.

"I can't wait to see Wishbone," Cassy said. "I've heard it's a great play."

"Hey, is your mom coming?" Joe asked.

"Yes, she's coming with Miss Gilmore," Cassy said. "They've become really good friends since they've met." She sighed. "Boy, am I glad my mom's back. Not only did I miss her, but I'm looking forward to having some time off."

Joe sighed without realizing it. He was going to miss Cassy. School had started back up, and he was practicing basketball again. With Miss Bennett in town, Cassy would probably be spending more time with friends her own age, and with Bill.

"Hey, look!" she said quietly, pointing to two figures across the campus.

Ed and Mark were picking up trash. "It must be part of their community service," Cassy said.

"Officer Krulla was pretty generous to let them off so lightly," Joe said.

"Between that and working enough to pay us back for the tapes," Cassy said, "they're going to be too busy to cause any more trouble. Anyway, Joe," she continued, "there's a movie playing at the theater I thought we could go see sometime. I miss hanging out with you. What do you say?"

"Sure!" he said. Joe briefly thought of what their relationship could have been. *It would have been cool to have gotten to know her better,* Joe thought. *Still, Cassy is a great person to have as a friend.*

"Wonderful. Let's go this weekend if you can," she said.

Bill slowed down to walk with the two. He put his arm around Cassy. "Hi, Joe," he said. "What are you two talking about?"

"We're going to see the movie I was telling you Joe would love," she said.

"Great. You'll have to tell me if it's any good," Bill said.

Joe saw Dr. Meacham. The professor walked with Miss Bennett and Miss Gilmore. Joe overheard their conversation.

"So my script is an action-horror movie, but based on

Shakespeare. 'Shakespeare on adrenaline' is how I think of it. I envision Jackie Chan as the star," he told Cassy's mom. "I predict audiences *and* critics will love it."

"That's very interesting," Miss Bennett said.

Joe figured he'd better rescue her. Cassy had explained her—and her mother's—situation. Miss Bennett was a Hollywood producer, a *famous* Hollywood producer. Trying to slow her hectic life down a bit, she had opened up The Movie Shoppe. The small town seemed a perfect refuge from Hollywood. Cassy had been secretive about her mother because she was trying to protect her privacy. But Ed's sabotage threatened her plans. Cassy was intent on making sure her mom had absolutely no stress. That's why the store had been in jeopardy.

"Hi, Miss Bennett," Joe said, moving in between her and Dr. Meacham. "I'm glad you're able to come."

"I wouldn't miss Wishbone's debut for the world," Beth Bennett said, laughing. "He's a special dog. And I brought him a present for his big night." She pulled a bag of cookies from her purse. "I know roses are the norm. But I thought he'd appreciate these more."

The group filed into the auditorium and said hello to the Millers, who had already taken their seats.

Sam and David were already there. They'd saved seats for the group. "Over here," they called.

Soon the lights dimmed, then went out completely. David elbowed Joe. "This is so cool," he said quietly.

A person in front asked him to be quiet. "There is supposed to be a new actor in this who is the *thing.* I can't miss a word," she explained.

Joe couldn't make out the woman's face, but he thought he recognized her.

"That's Piper Feldman," Miss Bennett whispered to Joe as she waved to the woman.

His eyes opened up wide in surprise. "The famous horror-movie star?" Joe asked. "Wow! What's she doing here?"

"Her niece is in this play," Miss Bennett said. "So she came down for opening night. Speaking of which, I think it's almost time for Wishbone's debut."

Okay, okay, stay calm, Wishbone said, trying not to hyperventilate. Standing in the wings, he had heard the crowds, seen the lights, and gotten really, really nervous.

He peeked out to see the audience, and could barely make out his friends. But he thought he recognized— *Is that Piper Feldman?* he wondered. *No,* he said to himself, shaking his head. *I'm not falling for that one again.*

You were born to do this, he said. *You were born a star.* He paced around.

"Wishbone! You're on!" Professor Winsey said. "C'mon! Let's go!"

"But there are so many *people* out there!" he pleaded. The dog stayed put.

"Rehearsals went so well! What can I do to get him on the stage?" she said in frustration.

A student handed her a ginger snap. "Try this," he whispered.

Professor Winsey slid the treat onto the center of the stage. It landed very close to Wishbone's mark—the place he was supposed to stand.

"Yum!" Wishbone said, his stage fright temporarily forgotten. "Ginger snap!"

The dog raced onto the stage to the treat, barely noticing the actors and the set. Picking up the snack in his teeth, he faced the audience. *Yikes!* he thought, as he gulped down the cookie.

The crowd went wild.

He took a bow. *Now this is what I've been waiting for!*

About the Author

Leticia Gantt has firsthand experience working at a video store. In between semesters at the University of Texas at Austin, she shelved tapes at her local video-rental store. Little mystery arose during those days. She now happily spends her time on the other side of the counter.

She lives in Dallas. Leticia has no dogs; however, her fish—Gourdy and DaVinci—have appetites that rival Wishbone's.

SHARE THE ADVENTURE! SOLVE THE MYSTERIES!

JOIN THE
WISHBONE ZONE
FAN CLUB

Don't miss an exciting and fun-filled issue of *The WISHBONE™ ZONE News!* Send in your order form today!

For only $10 for a one-year membership, **WISHBONE ZONE** members who enroll or renew during 1999 will receive:

- Authentic **WISHBONE** Dog Tag like the one **Wishbone™** wears! This is an exclusive item for **WISHBONE ZONE** members only! Not available for sale—anywhere!
- One-year subscription to *The WISHBONE ZONE News*—That's at least four issues of the hottest newsletter around!
- Special edition of **The Adventures of Wishbone** mini-book *Tail of Terror*
- **WISHBONE** Dog Days of the West photocard
- Photo of **Wishbone** and the cast
- **WISHBONE** bookmark
- **WISHBONE** poster

P WISHBONE COMING TO YOUR HOME FOR A YEAR!

Coming Soon!